DESERT AMBUSH

She didn't know how long she had been asleep when all hell broke loose. The sharp crack of a rifle shot furrowed the desert peace, followed by the louder, closer barking of pistols.

Disoriented and panicked, the world not yet in focus, Celia looked around for the source of the gunplay. It seemed to be coming from a slight ridge to her left.

A shot whistled by above her head as she began to slither forward over the ground, scrambling now to her feet as another bullet sizzled the air. Then from behind she heard the crunch of boots and the sickening click of a gun hammer being drawn back.

She whirled to face the single empty eye of death. The man who called himself Sam had a Colt .45 aimed straight at her heart . . .

TALES OF THE OLD WEST

SPIRIT WARRIOR   (1795, $2.50)
by G. Clifton Wisler
The only settler to survive the savage indian attack was a
little boy. Although raised as a red man, every man was his
enemy when the two worlds clashed—but he vowed no
man would be his equal.

IRON HEART   (1736, $2.25)
by Walt Denver
Orphaned by an indian raid, Ben vowed he'd never rest
until he'd brought death to the Arapahoes. And it wasn't
long before they came to fear the rider of vengeance they
called . . . Iron Heart.

WEST OF THE CIMARRON   (1681, $2.50)
by G. Clifton Wisler
Eric didn't have a chance revenging his father's death
against the Dunstan gang until a stranger with a fast draw
and a dark past arrived from West of the Cimarron.

BIG HORN GUNFIGHTER   (1975, $2.50)
by Robert Kamman
Quinta worked for both sides of the law, and he left a trail
of graves from old Mexico to Wyoming to prove it. His
partner cut and run, so Quinta took the law into his own
hands. Because the only law that mattered to a gunfighter
was measured in calibers.

BLOOD TRAIL SOUTH   (1349, $2.25)
by Walt Denver
John Rustin was left for dead, his wife and son butchered
by six hard-cases. Five years later, someone with cold eyes
and hot lead pursued those six murdering coyotes. Was it a
lawman—or John Rustin, himself?

*Available wherever paperbacks are sold, or order direct from the
Publisher. Send cover price plus 50¢ per copy for mailing and
handling to Zebra Books, Dept. 1994, 475 Park Avenue South,
New York, N.Y. 10016. Residents of New York, New Jersey and
Pennsylvania must include sales tax. DO NOT SEND CASH.*

POWELL'S ARMY

#1: UNCHAINED LIGHTNING

BY TERENCE DUNCAN

ZEBRA BOOKS
KENSINGTON PUBLISHING CORP.

ZEBRA BOOKS

are published by

Kensington Publishing Corp.
475 Park Avenue South
New York, NY 10016

First printing: February 1987

Printed in the United States of America

CHAPTER ONE

"The major from Washington City is here, sir," Lt. Col. Amos Powell's aide said, saluting crisply.

"Make him wait until 1405 hours," Amos instructed.

"Shall I tell him that, sir?"

"Certainly not," Powell snapped. Then, glaring up from his desk, he barked, "Dismissed."

The aide fled. Amos Powell was normally a stern but fair man, not given to bursts of temper. Powell was also a master tactician; he wanted the slight psychological edge over his visitor. He detested government politics, but he knew how to play the game.

So at precisely five minutes past the hour, the aide ushered Major Thaddeus Hurst into Amos' Fort Leavenworth office. The two men had known each other at West Point. Thaddeus had been called Pee Wee, a nickname bestowed without affection.

Amos now outranked his old adversary, but a major from Washington had more clout than any lieutenant colonel assigned to the U.S. Territorial Command of Kansas. Powell was not looking forward to the interview.

He rose to greet Major Hurst, shook his hand without warmth. "Should I be pleased about this visit?"

"I would think attention from Washington was always welcome," Thaddeus Hurst replied pompously. He also smirked. Amos recalled how much he had disliked the man even as a cadet.

"Perhaps it depends on who extends it, Major," Powell observed dryly.

Hurst ignored the implication. "Colonel Cuthbert suggested I pay you a call. He thought I might be able to pass on some friendly words of advice about that . . . undercover team of yours."

"Have a seat." Powell indicated a chair across from the broad oak desk, on which papers were aligned with military precision. Amos had suspected as much. He had been going over the files on his new operatives, searching for anything he might have missed.

Thus far, the official correspondence from Cuthbert had been positive, so he wondered about this visit. Visits from Washington were generally bad news.

Hurst, obviously, was relishing his role. He hrumphed and said slyly, "You know what some wags are calling your bunch of amateurs? Unofficially, of course?"

"Common sense?" Amos snapped. "After all, my team is going after cases the official army has been unable to solve, now that the funding has finally arrived."

"Yes, the funding. . . ." Hurst said, as if this gave him the upper hand. "I understand each of the three operatives is being paid $67.67 a month at a time when pay for the regular army has been reduced to $13 . . . in paper money."

"And the 'regular' army has been ineffective! My people will be laying their lives on the line every day."

"Perhaps," Major Hurst agreed, "but some people are wondering how effective an ex-Confederate, a girl barely

6

out of finishing school and an overeducated Indian will be—$67.67 a month effective? In fact, I have a little wager on it myself."

Bully for you, Pee Wee, Amos thought. He didn't have to ask on whose side the major had placed his bet. Amos pointedly consulted his watch and said, "I'm afraid I am pressed for time. Please state your business."

Hurst's face darkened with contained rage. He had been enjoying his little game. He and Amos Powell had been rivals back at West Point, and he had followed Amos' career with growing dismay, hoping the strong-willed man would fail.

"It seems the pressure is on Colonel Cuthbert," Thaddeus Hurst explained. "And, by extension, on you. There is, of course, the problem of budget I just mentioned. A review is coming up."

"How can they review something that hasn't had a chance to happen?" Amos protested. "My people are only now starting their first mission."

"Ah, yes," Thaddeus said, "the Fort Griffin affair. An unfortunate situation. Murder and mayhem—a distasteful business—that must be dealt with immediately. In fact, there is talk that if your people aren't one hundred percent effective, your entire project will be rescinded."

Amos knew better than to think they couldn't do that. This was a typical army maneuver. Funding today, and they wanted results yesterday. "And the reason for the rush?"

"The Western Cattle Trail. Making the West safe for commerce is always our most important consideration, don't you agree?"

It took great control for Amos to keep himself from groaning. *Damn the man.*

7

"And the citizens—voting citizens, that is—are trying to organize a county out there. Shackleford County, Texas, I believe. Dreadful name. Anyway, Fort Griffin is to be the county seat. So you see. . . ."

Amos saw, but that didn't mean he had to like it. "Just how much of a chance do my people get to prove themselves, before Washington withdraws its support?"

"I always knew you were a smart man," Thaddeus said. "Come up with concrete results within ninety days, or I'm afraid your little project is," he raised his hands in the air, empty palms up, "finished."

And that, Amos thought, would not only be a black mark against me, but would leave my operatives stranded, assuming they survived. He rose from his chair, indicating the interview was over. "If you have no more bad tidings. . . ."

"I guess that covers it," Thaddeus said. "Although Colonel Cuthbert approved the paperwork, he must have results. Soon. Just between us, of course."

"Of course," Amos replied smoothly. Unfortunately, he was recalling the telegram that had arrived yesterday, about the latest Fort Griffin murder. His effort to smile fell flat.

Instead, he again extended his hand, wishing he could let loose and punch Pee Wee Hurst in the mouth with it. "I will report to Colonel Cuthbert as soon as the first case is resolved," he said, exuding a confidence he did not feel. "In the meantime, extend my regards to him."

Before reaching the door, Major Hurst turned, wanting to get in the last word, and said, "Don't you want to know what the Washington brass are calling your team?"

"If you insist," Amos said.

"Powell's Army," Hurst laughed, as if it were a rare joke at the lieutenant colonel's expense. "Powell's Army."

Amos Powell did not laugh. He knew what the army could be like, the back-biting, the politics, the rule books. In spite of it, the army was Powell's life, and he believed in it. He also believed in the undercover team he had created, with one exception: the regular army liaison officer who had been thrust on him.

Once again, as he reviewed his folder, he grew angry recalling how much Thaddeus had known about this top secret information. He fervently hoped the leaks began, and ended, in Washington City.

At this very moment, Operative *C* should be meeting with Operatives *A* and *B* for the first time in Abilene, before the three of them headed south through the Indian Nations to Fort Griffin in the Department of Texas. Amos Powell had done everything in his power to protect their covers.

Second Lt. Preston K. Fox, the fourth member of the team, was also on his way there, in the company of a military convoy. Fox knew what the others looked like, had met them briefly some months ago.

Fox was a problem, which Amos hoped he had effectively neutralized by assigning him to a Fort Griffin post, rather than as an operative.

Dammit all, Amos thought as he reviewed his folder, *I hope my hunches are right. I hope they can win. I hope all of us can win.*

*   *   *

To: Col. R. A. Cuthbert
Adjutant General, U.S. Army
Washington City, D.C.

From: Lt. Col. Amos Powell
Adjutant General
U.S. Army Territorial Command
Fort Leavenworth, Kansas

Request authority to employ three civilian operatives to develop information for the Territorial
Command Adjutant General. These operatives—
one female, if possible—will function in situations
where regular U.S. Army inquiry proves fruitless,
and will include such matters as whiskey trade to
the tribes, control of businesses of ill repute
adjacent to posts and camps, reservation mutinies,
payroll or other theft, enlisted-personnel mutiny,
civilian disobedience of military regulation (such as
the current rush to Black Hills gold fields through
Sioux treaty land) and similar cases.

Request budget for above authority: $1,200 per
annum salary for each of above skilled operatives;
$5,000 per annum to cover expenses incurred in the
line of duty.

Request authority to transfer to Adjutant General
Command one lower-grade regular army officer to
be field supervisor of operatives. He will have
authority to make military arrests and to have other
policing powers per U.S. Army Code.

Jan. 4, 1874   POWELL

To: Lt. Col. Amos Powell, Adj. Gen.
Fort Leavenworth Territorial Command
Kansas

1. Authority to hire three civilian operatives granted.
2. Authority to recruit U.S. Army junior officer for requested duty granted.
3. Budget request modified as follows. Salary at $800 per annum per operative authorized. Expense money of $3,000 per annum authorized. It is expected that the operatives will utilize the hospitality of army posts and camps and employ army transport wherever possible.

Jan. 27, 1874   CUTHBERT

Confidential Dossier
Adjutant General Office
Fort Leavenworth

Disclosure of material in this dossier to unauthorized parties is grounds for general court-martial.

(Notes taken immediately following employment interview by Amos Powell.)

OPERATIVE *A*, code. CELIA LOUISE BURNETT. B. 1853 dtr of the late Capt. A.B. Burnett and Maria Chatsworth Burnett, deceased. A young lady of extraordinary comeliness, abt 5'6", red-haired, green-eyed, lightly freckled. An officer's child, familiar with army life and cynical about it. Parents killed in Oregon Trail massacre by Sioux near Ft. Laramie. Miss Burnett is a young lady of impeccable virtue, but daring and adventuresome and willing to plunge into situations that would repel a woman of reputation. Liability: sharp tongue, mocking tone. Liability: so outstandingly beautiful she will be widely noticed, which will jeopardize her undercover status. Assets: skilled at pianoforte, singing, poker, faro (can deal). Raised as a horsewoman. Familiar with small arms. No known romances, but is flirtatious. Has left broken hearts in her wake. Unusual education. After parents' death, raised by aunt in Waltham, Mass. Attended Miss Parsons' Finishing School. Fluent French. Rather worldly: alluded to bawdy soldier song during interview. Overall assessment: Highly valuable as operative. Highly vulnerable; will need protecting and supervision.

OPERATIVE *B*, code. GERALD GLIDINGHAWK, full-blooded Omaha raised by missionaries. B. 1851, Neb. Ter. Foster parents Methodists. Educated Glidinghawk for ministry, sent him to Dartmouth. Grad. Lib. Arts, Eng. Lit. major. Fluent Spanish, French, three Indian dialects—Omaha, Sioux, Nez Perce. Does not like white world, but unable to return to tribal life. Of two minds about this position, viz. dealing with subdued tribes. Amoral in spite of upbringing. Had half-breed common-law wife three years. Abandoned her and child. Has natural frontier and wilderness skills— horses, tracking, hunting, arms, etc. Bitter: fre-

12

quently banned from white saloons, eateries. This position is plainly a desperate livelihood rather than a career choice. Liability: loyalty questionable. Could be of great value in such matters as whiskey trade to tribes. Needs watching. Might respond to frequent commendation.

OPERATIVE *C*, code. LANDRUM DAVIS, B. 1833, San Antonio, Texas, Mexico. Civil War CSA Capt. Cavalry, Texas Second, wounded Memphis. Postwar, Texas Ranger, cited, meritorious service. Deep experience on frontier. Expert in all forms of military life—arms, strategy and tactics, horses, supervision, Indians, etc. Middle-aged, but fit and slim. Brown hair, graying. Brown eyes. Sabre scar across cheek. Bullet wounds thigh and buttock. Boasts of "Minie ball in the ass." Audacious but not reckless. Bad temper; got hot in interview when Civil War issues raised. Present loyalty probably acceptable. Tall, thin, strong shoulders, hawk nose. Eyes have piercing quality. Obviously must be made the senior of the three operatives. Natural leader. Minimal formal education. Speaks Comanche, some Spanish. Liability: might go too far, push too hard for information. Capable of torture or abuse. Has poor curb on emotions and appetites. Single, known to womanize. Must warn him about tampering with Operative *A*.

PRESTON KIRK FOX, RA, Second Lt. West Point Class of 1874; first posting. Age 21. Very young for such a sensitive and responsible assignment.

Would prefer a more exp. officer. Could jeopardize lives through inexperience. Will need to have West Point beaten out of him. He'll deal with civilians and with frontier situations not in the rule books. Will have sole authority to make arrests or issue policing orders, since others are civilians. He will need tact; may be arresting superior officers. Spit-and-polish now, but we shall see. Tentative assignment; sent to me over my protests. Middle of class, WP. Tends to be dogmatic, likely to be headstrong, hard to persuade to alter course when needed. A prig; has met Agent *A*, calls her a fallen woman. Has met Agents *B* and *C*, and expresses dismay at their alleged incompetence, looseness, and lack of discipline. Has little knowledge of the law or investigation of evidence. Liability: likely to condescend to all civilians and Indians. Will succeed only if Davis and I can pound some sense into him. Sees world in blacks and whites instead of frontier grays. Likely to be hell on Indians and unfortunates. Hate to have him in the field superior to Davis.

To: Operatives *A*, *B*, *C*
From: AP

If you were under arms, these would be your orders. You are civilians and these are your instructions. Treat them as orders.

The adjutant general is the administrative branch

of the army and also its policing branch. You will be gathering evidence leading to court-martial; gathering evidence against the civilian suppliers for the army who are defrauding us; dealing with Indian affairs, site selection of posts, civilian theft of army material and payroll, and so forth. Your operations will cover all the unsettled Western territories under the Fort Leavenworth Territorial Command as well as Western states now in the Union, such as California.

You have been employed as undercover operatives because normal military inquiry has often proved fruitless. Should you be exposed as an adjutant general operative at any time, your services to us would terminate. Your value lies in your acting incognito. Your field commander, Second Lieutenant Preston K. Fox, is the only one among you empowered by the Military Code to make arrests of military personnel. If you have information of interest to civilian authorities, take it to Lt. Fox, who will pass it along at his discretion. Never deal with civilian authorities yourselves—your cover may be destroyed.

Arm yourselves according to preference, but not with military issue. You may use your weapons in defense of life and limb and property, but not for arrest or detainment of military personnel.

You will be supplied with papers identifying you as AG operatives, but these are to be shown only *in extremes.* They are to be secreted on your persons in such places as hollow heels or in a hatband. If you should be forced to reveal your true mission and authority—for instance, to avoid execution by a military firing squad—your services to us would be necessarily terminated.

Lt. Fox will on some occasions function openly as an inspecting officer of the AG; at other times, incognito as Operative *D*. You must never be seen consulting with him when he is openly an active AG officer.

Your service will be perilous at all times. The military has its share of felons and violent men and mountebanks. Your only reward will be the gratitude of the United States Army and your servant,

POWELL

Amos Powell sighed. Landrum Davis should be handing these instructions around right now. Davis was a good man, and if anyone could pull the operatives together as a working unit, he could.

It should be interesting. For a moment, Amos felt a pang of regret that he had long since retired from field work. The challenge, he knew, was continually working with the unexpected—a far different thing than receiving reports post facto.

Before completing his review, Lt. Col. Amos Powell reread the dispatch concerning Fort Griffin and the

Flats. He attached the telegram about the latest murder to the folder. It was too bad he could not send on the news of the latest murder to his operatives. But they would find out about it soon enough.

Powell's Army, he thought, rather liking the name even as he recalled the smug grin on Hurst's face. *May victory be yours.*

CHAPTER TWO

Celia Louise Burnett froze in mid-step on Texas Street, outside the Bull's Head Saloon. She twisted up the long serge skirt of her traveling suit in her fist. It had been threatening to drag on the muddy ground.

From beyond the batwing doors, she heard a piano player banging out tinny notes, the tune unfamiliar. A cowboy rather than a soldier song, she thought. Loud curses of losing gamblers, muffled laughter; the shrill shriek of a honky-tonk woman rounded out the cacophony.

Riveted to the street, she stared past the unshaven, loitering men and *nymphs du prairie,* who blinked like newborn pink mice in the light of day. She had seen the likes of them before.

But she had never seen the likes of the crude painting, the subject of which appeared to be charging from the false-front building. It was, appropriately, of a bull—an extremely graphic bull whose most bullish feature was painted over, though the outline of the salient anatomical feature remained.

A blush crept from the neckline of her dress and moved in quickening currents across her face, finally becoming lost in her thick red mane. Her complexion, fair and lightly dusted with freckles, was left a rosy pink in its wake. In spite of wrangling her way into a job as a secret agent for the army, Celia still couldn't believe Lt. Col. Amos Powell had summoned her, a single woman only twenty-one years old, for this work.

She tried to tear her eyes away from the painted bull's monstrous equipment. Abilene was, after all, only a foretaste of the wild and wicked places she would see on her new job. She had been instructed to meet her fellow operatives here.

Celia had arrived from St. Louis on the Central Pacific Railroad the day before, as per instructions. The message from Fort Leavenworth told her to wait at the Drovers' Cottage, a nice hotel, although it was the rest of Abilene that drew her like sin sermons draw bands of the righteous.

Taking in the sights of the raw boom town had not been mentioned in the telegram. Celia suspected her actions might be frowned upon. But Celia had a mind of her own—a stubborn streak, her late father had called it—and she figured her job did not officially begin until she met with Operatives *B* and *C* and received her first assignment.

She was disappointed that she was to meet the two men with whom she was to work undercover—a term that thrilled her—at the hotel. It did not fit her growing sense of adventure. She would have liked to meet at one of the saloons. Abilene had scores of them.

Celia glanced past the louvered doors of the Bull's Head to the green-felt-covered gambling tables inside. Celia loved faro and was a better-than-average dealer of the game. That was something she had not learned at

Miss Parsons'.

Her hands itched to play, to slap down the cards on the betting board, to hear the clink of chips as the winning bets were called. She was fighting the temptation to enter the place—knowing it would not be wise for a woman who wanted to remain inconspicuous—when suddenly a tall Indian was manhandled out the front door by an unwashed cowboy.

"And don't try to come back to no white man's place," the angry man slurred as he catapulted the Indian through the air to land in a heap at Celia's feet, dragging her skirt down into a puddle. Celia recoiled. Moments before, she had seen a tobacco-chewing youth spit in the same puddle.

The bully lunged forward, stomping on Celia's skirt, and made a move to grab the Indian's shirt collar. The red man growled, baring teeth as white as new snow. A flash of pure venom as swift and elusive as a lightning bolt crossed his snarling face. Then his expression closed up, hard and impassive as carved stone.

The man with the beefy, outstretched fists had seen the face of a savage beast, though, and had recognized the murderous warning.

He also heard Celia's sharp voice addressing him. "If you dare molest this man, I will scream for the sheriff," she said. "And now, will you get off my skirt?"

The cowboy, inwardly relieved by the lady's intercession, mumbled incoherently and backed off, sidling back in to the saloon. Celia was still rooted to the spot by the man lying in the mud.

She waited for him to move, expecting an illiterate grunt of gratitude and hoping he would not slaver. She had, she thought, averted a nasty fight.

"Pardon me, ma'am," the Indian said, lying woodenly, staring up. "I believe we are both the victims of an aggrieved loser."

He gestured as if tipping his hat, but he wore none. His hair was the deep, shiny black of anthracite coal. His eyes were of the same intense blackness. Celia realized he was an extremely handsome man.

The stranger coiled his sprawled limbs and jumped to his feet like an oiled spring. He dusted off his broadcloth britches. His eastern clothes hung well on him. Penetrating eyes surveyed Celia boldly.

Damn him! She found herself blushing again as he took in the fiery color of her hair, the emerald green of her eyes and the lithe tallness of her figure.

"Enjoying the sights?" he asked, gazing at the bull's painted-over appendage. In profile, the man's nose was distinctive, with a pronounced hook at the bridge. Set prominently in his lean, bronzed face, all he would have needed was a feathered headdress to make him look like the engraving on a coin.

Celia supposed he was several years older than herself. Faint squint lines around his eyes made him look as if he had spent a lot of time outdoors.

Celia had never known an Indian who spoke like a white man and, while she couldn't quite place the accent, it sounded vaguely familiar to her New England-attuned ears. His cultured voice could not mask the boldness of his speech.

She searched her memory for the advice drummed into her by the *Social Mirror*—a bible of manners for young ladies that had been forced on her at Miss Parsons'— about putting strangers firmly in their place. Her mind came up blank.

The Indian had a certain aplomb for someone who had just been kicked out of a saloon by a rowdy drunk. In spite of herself, Celia admired it. She hoped she could act as cool in the face of adversity.

"Would you, by any chance, be Celia?" he asked.

"Miss Burnett," Celia replied automatically.

"Landrum Da. . . . Rather, I should say Operative *C* has been looking for you. He will meet you at the Drovers' Cottage in half an hour. We will go over our orders and leave Abilene tomorrow."

Suddenly, Celia was mortified. We? That meant this Indian was one of them. *One of us,* she corrected herself. He had not only seen her gawking at the famous saloon front, but his manner was mocking, as if the secrecy, the code names, were so much hogwash.

Celia, too, was often cynical about the army's way of doing things, but she took her new job seriously. It was not every day a woman got a chance to work at something exciting. This Indian irked her.

"I'll report there immediately," Celia said, hating the prissy edge to her words.

She turned on her heels and walked away, shoulders squared, head in the air. From behind her, she heard his mock whisper, ". . . and don't tell anyone."

Celia's first, fleeting impression of Landrum Davis was of a man accustomed to being obeyed. His military bearing was as apparent as his Southern accent when he rose to greet her.

He was tall, spare, his carriage erect. When he bowed to her—though she could tell it pained him, irritated him beneath the automatic politeness—his manner was courtly.

Courtly was not what Celia had hoped for—not this gentlemanly greeting. It set her apart as a lady, not a compatriot.

Gerald Glidinghawk, the Indian, also rose and bowed. Somehow, his stilted gesture carried an overtone of ridicule which Celia pointedly ignored.

"You two have met, I take it?" Davis said. "Good, then we can skip the formalities. Go ahead and sit down. I want each of you to read the dispatches from Lieutenant Colonel Amos Powell, then we can talk."

Celia's skirts rustled as she seated herself at the conference table in the back room of Abilene's most luxurious hotel. It was a room that had seen many thousand head of beef change hands. A round mahogany table was flanked by captain's chairs and illuminated by an overhead chandelier.

It was a businesslike, no-nonsense room, permeated by the odor of the good cigars that had been smoked there. A man's room.

Celia was pleased to be between the two men. She detested being herded in with giggling, empty-headed females, especially when she knew she could ride and shoot as well as most men, and had a sharp mind as well. That was one of the reasons she had wanted this job. She was, she supposed, proud to be part of this team.

She had imagined these men would be different, though. She had thought that the Indian would look more like the scouts she had seen on army posts, who dressed in breechclouts, not broadcloth, and spoke in guttural monosyllables.

And Landrum Davis' accent threw her. She had been expecting the hard vowels of a career officer, not the slow, honeyed speech of a renegade former Confederate. She was sure that was what he was, judging from his ramrod stiff bearing and his manner. Men born and bred south of the Mason-Dixon Line acted differently from other men.

Celia tried to put these thoughts from her mind and read the dispatches from Colonel Powell. The three of them would just have to accept each other, respect each other, if they were to work together.

She hoped neither man noticed the faint trembling of her slender fingers as she began to realize just what she had gotten herself into. Suddenly, this was no longer a wild and daring adventure, no longer a schoolgirl prank like thumbing her nose at convention.

The first dispatch minced no words. Celia stifled a wild impulse to giggle as she thought of hiding her top secret papers in the heel of her shoe . . . or perhaps in another, more obvious place. This was real—and deadly serious.

The second dispatch, about their first mission together, made that perfectly clear. It read:

To: *A, B, C*
From: Lt. Col. Amos Powell
Adjutant General, U.S. Army
U.S. Army Territorial Command
Fort Leavenworth, Kansas

You are directed to the vicinity of Fort Griffin, Texas. Near that camp, in a notorious area known as the Flats, are several establishments known to enlisted men as, alas, pigpens. These cater to all manner of vices. In recent months, three enlisted men have been coldly murdered there, numerous others knifed or drugged. A quarter of the command has been systematically rolled, bilked or robbed of monthly payroll.

Complaints to Texas civil authorities have accomplished nothing. Placing various establishments off-limits has also accomplished nothing. It is believed that a powerful ring of madams and grogshop operators is bribing Texas officialdom (and possibly officers at the fort—an aspect you will have to investigate). Your assignment is to gather information leading to possible courts-martial at Fort Griffin, to develop information to turn over to high Texas officials, and to devise ways and means to bring the Flats under control. It is suggested that Operative *A* employ her skills as a faro dealer to acquire further information.

At present, Fort Griffin is only fifty percent effective because of the abuses at the Flats. Caution: The denizens of the Flats are animals and barbarians, reckless of life and health, and absolutely dangerous.

Celia finished reading and handed it to Gerald Glidinghawk. In the ensuing silence, she could feel Landrum Davis studying her. She pasted a calm expression across her face—the same one she had used to conceal things from the aunt who had finished raising her, the same look that had fooled her mistresses at school.

It did not seem to fool Davis. Celia made a conscious effort to keep her brow uncreased and her lips set in a loose line, neither frowning nor smiling. She forced herself to breathe in a measured rhythm. She was, she thought, good at hiding her true feelings. But Davis, she was afraid, saw right through her, saw the fear mixed with her excitement.

Glidinghawk was scowling at the papers in fierce concentration. Celia wondered if he had trouble reading swiftly, then silently chided herself. Glidinghawk might make her uncomfortable—as Davis was doing now—but he had all the marks of an educated man.

The silence and the tension were growing unbearable. Celia was aware of how uncomfortably tight her corset was—she hated the blasted things—and of the weight of the tiny derringer slipping from her garter. She had armed herself before walking through Abilene. And although she knew that from more than five feet away a derringer was about as useful as tits on a bull—another expression she had not learned around Boston—it had made her feel safer.

If it came clattering out of her garter now, Davis would probably think her a real ninny. In fact, she was getting the feeling he and the Indian already felt that way. She should have known it would be like this.

Damn. Her petticoats swished as she reached down, as if she desperately needed to scratch an itch. It was not a ladylike act, but understandable. She started to adjust her small weapon more securely.

At that exact moment, Celia heard the click of another gun being cocked. Past Glidinghawk's bowed head, she saw the door to the conference room open a crack.

She reacted instinctively. Her pearl-handled revolver flashed in her hand. She was fast. She aimed and fired before her brain fully registered the glint of a Colt .45

muzzle pointing in Glidinghawk's direction.

Her shot splintered wood.

"Dammit all!" she grunted. She hurled herself forward into a half-crouch, steadied her gun arm on her knee and squeezed off another shot. This one shattered bone.

A big man bellowed in pain. His gun clattered to the floor, followed by his flailing body. He lay there clutching the gushing red fingers of his empty gun hand, bewildered.

Dazed, in pain, he looked stupidly up at Celia. He had been sure neither of the men had spotted him. He could not comprehend that she had shot the gun right from his hand.

The acrid smell of cordite stung the air. Davis was on his feet, staring down through the curling haze of blue-black smoke.

"Who the hell is this?" he swore softly, looking from the wounded cowboy to Celia, and back to the downed man again.

Celia recognized the injured man as the same one who had earlier thrown Glidinghawk out of the Bull's Head. She offered no resistance when Davis took the tiny, smoking pistol from her hand.

"I'll be damned," he finally said.

"I'm afraid I am responsible for this," Gerald said. "I was quite successful in a game of poker earlier today, and this man demanded his money back because I was an Indian playing in a white man's game."

Celia noted Glidinghawk's proud, flaring nostrils in an otherwise blank face. She realized what the iron control must cost him.

"I allowed the man to throw me out of the gambling

hall without fighting back. It went against my nature . . . but I didn't want any personal problems to reflect on our mission, sir."

"The name's Landrum," Davis said, dropping his earlier tone of reserve. "We aren't exactly regular army, are we? Let's have the marshal drag this scoundrel out of here and start all over again." He turned to Celia. "That was some nice shooting, even though I don't set much stock in derringers."

Davis shouted for the desk clerk, who came running on small feet. He was a crinkled man with a pasty face and thin, no-color hair.

"Get this piece of garbage out of here," Davis ordered him. "I thought Abilene was becoming civilized."

The clerk stammered, "We don't allow gun-slinging riffraff on the premises. I'll fetch Marshal Hickok. These things do not happen at the Drovers' Cottage."

"Really?" Davis did not have to say more. He kicked the door shut, splintering more wood. "At least this has nothing to do with our mission."

He glared at Celia and Glidinghawk, as if defying them to contradict him. Then he focused on the Indian. "So, you were gambling, passing time in a saloon?"

"All Indians drink and gamble if they get a chance, don't they, sir?" The downward twist to Gerald's mouth was more revealing than his words. Davis could not miss it.

"Don't get your dander up," he said curtly. "I'm not against gambling, drinking, or womanizing, as long as none of them interfere with our orders. I imagine you and I will be called on to do all three—in the line of duty, of course. You did the right thing, not raising a ruckus then. You couldn't know he'd chase you down."

Gerald said simply, "Thank you, sir."

Davis nodded, seemingly lost in concentration. Then, he plunged in. "I've had some doubts about taking this job, about working with a—pardon me, ma'am—greenhorn woman and a savage—again, apologies. But it has nothing to do with you being a woman, or you an Indian."

Davis' commanding eyes darted from one to the other as he spoke. Celia expected that he was normally a taciturn man, but could tell that if he was provoked enough, he knew how to get things off his chest.

"I was told both of you have 'unique' qualifications," he continued, "and I must admit, I've never yet met a lady who was handy with a gun, or an Indian who didn't 'How' me to distraction. Now that I have, let's get down to work."

Celia lowered herself into her chair, hoping the others wouldn't notice how the incident had left her shaken. Though skilled and confident at target shooting, she had never before sent a bullet plunging into human flesh and bone. The move had been pure reflex.

Thank God she hadn't killed him. It would not do to have an attack of the vapors now, not when Davis and Glidinghawk had seen she could be valuable to them.

"Are you all right, ma'am," Glidinghawk asked. The mockery was gone. She had just, very probably, saved his life. Indians were the ones who were supposed to see and hear everything that happened behind their backs. The irony was not lost on him.

"I think I need a shot of whiskey," Celia said. After all, wasn't that what a man who had just shot somebody would ask for?

CHAPTER THREE

Davis ceremoniously poured their last shots of whiskey into tin cups—a full shot for Celia and himself, and a few token drops for Glidinghawk. Gerald had admitted that, like most Indians, he didn't mix well with firewater. He drank sparingly.

Davis eyed his colleagues with a strange smile across his thin lips. The ride to Texas had bonded them as only cold, rough nights on the trail can. Perhaps Amos Powell had thought of that when he suggested it as the fastest route to Fort Griffin.

Glidinghawk was now dressed in the butter-soft, worn buckskins and moccasins of a Plains Indian. Celia wore trousers and a slouch felt hat that protected her fair complexion and hid her flaming tresses. Davis was decked out in stiffer, fringed buckskins, befitting a buffalo hunter.

"To our mission," Celia said, raising her cup. "And hot-water baths, soft beds and meals without beans. . . ."

"Shhh . . . ," Gerald cautioned, cocking his head and listening to the night sounds. Celia heard the horses whinny and the fire crackle. In the distance, a wolf howled.

"Indians?" Landrum asked. Although they had passed through the Indian Nations without incident, in this part of northeast Texas, untamed bands of Kiowas still roamed freely.

Gerald put his ear to the ground, listened intently. "Not unless they've taken to shoeing their horses. White men, I would guess."

"How many?"

"Hard to tell. More than one horse, but not enough for a gang." Desperadoes also roved here, usually on their way to the lawless No Man's Land to the north.

The muffled beat of horses' hooves was now apparent, even to Celia's untrained ear. So far, luck had been with them. This would be an awful time for their luck to change. It was their final camp.

Right now, from a distance, Celia looked like an adolescent boy. Tomorrow, she would resume her identity as a woman and catch the stage for the last leg of her journey into Fort Griffin. Davis and Glidinghawk were to ride in separately.

"Let's hope they are friendly—and dumb," Davis said. He reached over and fingered an errant lock of Celia's long hair as if it were spun glass. He tucked it back under the brim of her dark hat.

She started, surprised at the gentleness of his touch and the mixed message it conveyed. Celia reminded herself that Landrum was almost old enough to be her father and, thus far, seemed to accept her as one of the team.

"It wouldn't do for a stranger to catch on we have a woman here," he told her. "Keep your hat down and don't talk."

Glidinghawk had been watching the interplay between

32

Celia and Davis, his face a carved mask. It was almost impossible for Celia to tell what he was thinking.

The approaching men looked like ghost riders in the muted blue moonlight. There were two of them, slowing now as they neared camp. They had been riding hard. Moonglow illuminated the sweating flanks of their mounts.

The one in the lead reined in and halted fifty yards from them. He held his right hand at the ready, near his holster.

Davis stood tall. The long barrel of his Winchester rifle glinted metallically as he raised it, aiming in the strangers' direction. "Friend or foe?" he called out.

A raucous snort from the second man caused Glidinghawk to motion silently and emphatically to Celia. She swallowed her resentment at being pointed at like a trained dog and edged her way toward the horses and bedrolls.

"As friendly as you'll let us be," the first man shouted. "We'd like to share your camp."

From closer in, the men looked as dusty and unwashed as one would expect from the trail. The first was a burly fellow with a dark, unkempt beard. The second was shorter, but stout, his beady eyes set in a porcine face.

Davis and Glidinghawk exchanged a quick look. They were thinking alike. Neither stranger looked like a good bedfellow, but having them close by might be a damned sight better than watching out for them through the long night.

"Come'n then," Davis said. He put down the Winchester but kept it within reaching distance.

The first man, the spokesman, dismounted. "I guess it pays to be careful around these parts." There was a wary quickness to his eyes, a gruff rasp to his voice.

Davis grunted, "Especially of strangers riding hard in the dark of night."

The stranger extended his hand. "Name's Sam. Sam Taggart. My partner here calls himself The Kid. We're after some bandits, stole some of our horses. You see a gang, about five horses in tow, further north?"

"Didn't see anyone but some Indians, up in the Nations," Landrum said. He acted as if his guard was lowered. By now, both Celia and Gerald knew better.

"Folks call me Landrum, and that there," he pointed to Celia who was obscured by the shadows, "is my son Bo. Got some sickness, can't talk much. Son, you get yourself bedded down, you hear?"

Celia heard. She hated to spend her last night on the trail like this, but she curled herself into the bedroll— just her and the Peacemaker she had been practicing with earlier today—and pretended to settle down.

"And the Indian?" the one who called himself Sam asked with a snarl. "He yours?"

"You might say," Davis answered. "What's it to you?"

"Me and The Kid hate Indians, is all. Could've been some Indians riding with the gang that stole our horses. Indians are good at them things. I'd watch it if I were you, mister, riding with a red man."

"Oh, I do," Davis replied laconically. "He's a pretty good lookout, though. Eyes and ears in back of their heads, these Indians. Don't need much sleep, either."

Both Sam and The Kid—who didn't look so much like a kid as a sawed-off buscadero—got the message.

They were spreading their bedrolls as Celia drifted, lulled by the gruff, muted tones of the men's talk. She was not taken in by the strangers, but she figured all of them were caught in an uneasy truce.

Besides, there was nothing Celia could do, and she was tired. The ride had been long and hard, but she had kept up without complaint. She had also slept better than she could ever recall, even on the uncushioned ground.

Back in Abilene, when Celia had pitted her derringer against the sore loser, that had been a lucky shot. Pure luck. On the trail, she felt she had earned her place as part of the team.

She, Davis and Glidinghawk had become adept at reading each other's signals. After the first few days, their riding pace had meshed nicely, too. Celia had faith in Landrum and Gerald, faith that they had tonight's situation covered.

And neither stranger had gotten a good look at her or become curious. Even the thought of parting from the others in the morning, of taking on her cover as a gambling gal, could not help Celia fight the weight of her eyelids.

She didn't know how long it was until all hell broke loose. She heard the sharp crack of a rifle shot echo furrow the peace. It was followed by the louder, closer barking of pistols. She woke in a hurry.

The fire had smoldered out. Pre-dawn light had turned the sky a dull, lead gray. She looked around for Landrum and Gerald, for the source of the gunplay. It sounded like it was coming from behind a slight ridge to her left.

Davis' large gelding, Lone Star, nickered and pawed the ground. Celia swung her wild gaze to the animal. She was disoriented, wide awake now, but panicked. The world had not yet come into sharp focus.

But the horses seemed to be in a different position

from where they were before she had gone to sleep. She saw her own mount back away, untethered, and quickly slid from her blankets like a snake, leaving the heavy Peacemaker. She moved to secure the horses.

Another shot whistled by above her head, but she could not see where it had come from. She slithered forward, scrambling now on her knees, hands outstretched to get to the animals before they bolted.

"Hey, boy. Hey, Lone Star," she called, mustering a calm she did not feel. She knew horses—another subject she didn't learn at school, but from her cavalryman father—and she knew that the next few seconds were crucial.

She willed herself forward inch by inch as another bullet sizzled the air. She called to the edgy animals, making her quaking voice soothing. Lone Star was the key. If she could grab his bridle, the others should follow. Like his master, he had automatically taken his position as leader.

From the corner of her eye, Celia saw a man top the ridge and catapult into the air before flopping down in a splatter of blood and guts. She strained to keep her eyes forward, addressing the horse she was desperately wooing.

The horses saw the man fall and they bucked at the gun's retort—except for Lone Star, whose eyes were locked with Celia's. The gelding was almost within reach. One more inch, then another, and Celia plunged forward, grabbed his reins and tugged as his forelegs pawed the air.

Lone Star battled Celia, bucking with fright. His whinny sounded like a human shriek. Woman and beast fought. Celia's grip was tighter than a hangman's noose. Leather dug into her fingers.

Glidinghawk's small mustang took off in a gallop, but Celia's mount nudged Lone Star, eyes rolling over white, terrified, undecided. With the last of her strength, Celia grabbed her bridle as well.

Celia had two of the horses. Two out of three.

From behind her, she heard the crunch of boots on earth and the sickening click of a gun hammer being drawn back. Her breath was coming out in ragged gasps from the fear and exertion.

She whirled around to face the single empty eye of death. The man who called himself Sam had a Colt .45 aimed right at her.

"Hold it steady, lad," Sam said. "Or is it lady?"

Oh my God, Celia thought. The hat had fallen off her head. Her trousers and shirt were ripped, her face streaked with dirt. But even the red-clay dust could not hide her long mane of flaming hair.

Where was Gerald? Landrum? Who was the man who had fallen? She needed to reassure herself that it was not one of them. Celia craned her neck and looked.

No, he was a man Celia had never set eyes on before. Or he had been a man, before the large caliber bullet tore a gaping hole through his middle. He was sprawled on his back, his limbs stretched out at odd angles like a broken doll. His eyes stared blankly skyward, not seeing the new day dawning. Not seeing anything.

Celia knew she was going to be sick. She had never seen a dead man before, not like this, so clear and vivid and fresh.

The door of her mind had slammed shut on the grisly scenes she had seen as a girl. The only dead people she could remember seeing were neatly laid out in a funeral parlor. They had not looked like this. Her stomach roiled.

"You just hand me them there reins, little lady," Sam said. Celia was too sick to notice how jittery he was. Wherever Landrum and Gerald were, it was too far.

Head spinning, Celia tried to think as she took a small, faltering step forward. Her bedroll—if only she could get to the Colt in her bedroll. But it was hopeless, with Sam's gun pointing straight at her heart.

Sam took a step forward. They faced each other, almost close enough to touch. Instinctively, she pulled back on the reins holding the two mounts. They had gentled down now, but their flanks still quivered.

Sam had the gun. She had the horses. If he shot now, she would drop the reins and the horses would scatter. It might give her a chance.

What had Landrum said about ambush, about horse thieves, about working together on the trail? So many lessons they had gone over, so many plans for emergencies, and now she could not think. She was going to throw up. She couldn't hold out—couldn't hold it in.

She stepped forward with the reins as bile gushed from her mouth. It spewed out like a fountain.

"Bitch!" Sam hissed. He sidestepped, gun wavering as he swiped at his face. Celia doubled over and retched again as a shot blasted her eardrums.

Time and distance played tricks. For an eternal heartbeat, Celia saw Glidinghawk bounding toward her as Sam stumbled backward, raised his gun, squeezed the trigger and fired blindly as he fell. It was as if his muscles kept moving in their deadly path while his heart and brain had stopped.

Glidinghawk cursed as the shot grazed his shoulder. He dove to the ground beside Celia and grabbed for the reins she still held in a vise grip. Her fingers were talons, stiff

38

and unyielding around the leather. He had to pry them off.

When she could raise her head again, Celia asked, "Landrum?"

"Out there. He should be here soon. There were four of them. Landrum wounded The Kid, but he got away. So did the other man. At least you saved two of the horses."

Celia was silent. She knew, now, that she should never have allowed herself to go to sleep. It was weak, womanly. Gerald's mustang was gone and they could have been in much worse shape.

Finally, Davis appeared from behind the ridge. His eyes were red-rimmed and weary. "I think that's it for now," he said. "What's the damage here?"

"I have a superficial wound in my humerus," Glidinghawk said.

"What the hell . . . is that supposed to be funny?" Landrum snorted. "If I get shot in the ass, I'll tell you I got shot in the ass—without any fancy college talk."

"A minor wound in the upper arm," Gerald said, holding his shoulder now. He did not flinch, though it must have hurt like the devil. "I'm afraid I was tired of all the Indian pow-wow talk last night, sir. I wasn't trying to be smart."

"None of us are," Davis said bitterly. "Are you going to need a sawbones?"

"I can take care of it the Indian way."

"The mustang's gone," Celia said. She felt she should be the one to report it. "It was my fault."

Now, after the fracas was over, she remembered Landrum's advice. She should have remained alert and fled with the horses at the first sign of trouble. "I'm sorry."

Davis nodded. "We didn't mean to go off and leave you, either. Two of those bastards came sneaking up from behind the ridge. We thought we were ready, but we were wrong. It happens. We didn't have time to warn you."

He looked at Celia's disheveled hair and streaked face. He saw that she had been violently ill. Perhaps she should not have slept, but she had learned her lesson—the hard way.

"Shall I make some coffee, Landrum?" Gerald asked.

"Go ahead, I think we all could use some. But I think it's going to take more than coffee to get Celia in shape to meet up with Ben Ficklin's Mail and Stage Line."

Both men looked at her.

Until now, it had been a blessedly uneventful trip. Celia had shrieked some, when they had discovered body lice in her bedding, but it had passed. She had come across as a real trouper.

Her next step was to assume the role of a traveling faro dealer seeking employment. She had to be sharp—and she had to be unknown. Suddenly, she felt far from ready.

"Landrum, when I heard those shots I forgot everything. I wasn't prepared. Maybe we should go over everything again. Maybe I'll pay more attention this time. I . . . I'm afraid I panicked as bad as the horses."

"Don't be too hard on yourself," Davis said. "Did The Kid or the other bastard get a look at you? Guess the two who died don't count."

"Not the one with the monicker . . . the other one did, before he ran," Gerald said. Celia had been too busy and too far away to see what had happened.

"Tarnation!" Landrum said. "He looked like a man I've seen somewhere . . . a crooked gambler. I guess it can't be helped. Let's just hope they head for No Man's Land and stay there."

Davis read the time in the rising sun. "Looks like we couldn't get you on stage today, even if you were ready. I hope this isn't a jinx."

It felt like it to Celia. Two men dead and they had not yet reached Fort Griffin. Both Gerald and Landrum seemed to take the incident as a matter of course in a wild and rugged land. Celia realized how foreign it was to her. She had thought she was tough and brave . . . until this.

"What are we going to do with . . . them?" she asked.

"I'm not too fond of digging, myself," Landrum said. "Let the vultures have them."

Celia shuddered.

She wondered if she could ever get used to this callous disregard for life. As she heard them make plans to track down the mustang that had fled, she realized that a horse had more value out here than the life of a man. Or perhaps, of a woman.

CHAPTER FOUR

While Glidinghawk went off to track his runaway mustang, Celia and Davis moved their makeshift camp two miles to the east, upwind of the corpses, near a swift stream. Swollen from the thaw, the waters ran a deep, rusty color, slick with the viscous red clay peculiar to the area. "If I don't get a bath pretty soon, I won't even want to be downwind of myself," Davis said.

"Landrum . . . don't you feel . . . well, awful, leaving those men to rot?" Celia asked, voicing the questions that had been bothering her. "What did they want from us? Why would anyone risk getting himself shot over a few horses?"

"Horses and guns," Landrum said. His eyes focused on a place far away, as if trying to remember what it was like when he saw his first man gunned down. "Out here, there's a lot of men who act like animals, who think they can be king of the heap. And they need to be shot down like animals."

"Doesn't that make you just like them?" Celia asked sharply. She knew there had been no choice in killing the men, but leaving their bodies for the vultures still rankled her.

"One big difference, and don't you forget it. We're trying to get rid of their kind. We are trying to make the West safe for men. Their kind is only out to grab what they can get. And they'll gun down any man, woman or child who stands in their way."

Celia shook her head. It sounded noble, but there had been nothing noble about seeing the guts spill out of Sam's wound. She wondered if she would ever understand why.

Landrum hadn't gotten much practice explaining the ways of the West, Celia could tell, and she appreciated the way he kept his voice calm, gentle. She couldn't help wondering if it was a strain for him.

"Killing us didn't mean any more to them than shooting rabbits, only the prize was better. Their horses were run ragged, ours were better. They figured us for easy pickings. Men like that don't think getting killed can happen to them. It's that simple."

"It scares me," Celia admitted.

"It should. The same thing can happen to us if we aren't careful. There are snakes out here, and there will be snakes in Fort Griffin. Only difference is, out here you know who they are. In there, it gets complicated."

"I'll be right in the middle of it, won't I?" Celia asked.

"Glidinghawk will be there, and I'll be in and out. But yes, you will be in the middle. I don't think you'll have to shoot anyone, but be prepared. Once you get set up working in a saloon, I figure you will be our main source of information."

"Shall we go over it again?" Celia asked.

"Quickly. You are in a saloon dealing faro. I come to your table and lay a bet on the queen. What do you do?"

"I pretend I don't know you. I take your bet and work

44

out the rest of the night. Then I leave—on the alert for you or Gerald to give me further instructions. I'm in trouble, but I still have some time. . . ."

"Good," Landrum said. "And if I copper my bet on the queen?"

"I make some excuse—any excuse—and run like hell. I'm in immediate danger."

"Good girl," Landrum approved. "The first law out here is self-preservation."

"What if I don't get hired?" Celia asked. The codes were fine, the methods they had worked out, but that part of the mission seemed very far away.

"You think they will turn down a woman dealer out here? That's the beauty of your cover. Gambling gals have a way of showing up out of nowhere. And they are worth more than gold to these saloon owners."

"How do I know which saloon to go to work at? What if I get it wrong?"

"First, you ride in on the stage. Glidinghawk will get you to the outpost and disappear. You don't owe anyone explanations. You buy yourself a ticket to the Flats. You rent yourself a room. You ask around. People are always eager to talk about killings . . . it's the way things are. Then, from what you pick up, you go to the most likely saloon and—"

"I'm not a child," Celia protested. "I know all that. But look, my hands are all beat up." She held them up, so Davis could see the raw scars left from holding the panicked horses. "People are bound to ask questions. And how the hell can I deal a good game with hands like these?"

Landrum's patience was exhausted. His brown eyes flashed with irritation. "If you have any doubts, we'll get

45

you on a stage headed back east. Sure, a lot of things are uncertain. You might end up working the wrong saloon. You might get shot at, beat up . . . or worse. You don't think you can handle it, get out right now."

Celia was also riled. "I didn't say I couldn't handle it." Her chin jutted up defiantly.

Davis scowled at her. "Maybe I wish you would turn around and go home. I've seen a lot of men die. Women too. The war . . . the Texas Rangers . . . it's not an easy life out here. Why any fool woman would choose to work as an undercover agent is beyond me. And I'm the one who will be responsible for you."

Horse's hooves thundered into camp. Glidinghawk was back, just in time to pull Celia back from saying something she knew she'd regret.

She stood up abruptly and ran toward Glidinghawk, smiling. He had recaptured his mustang and had a slew of cottontails for dinner slung over his saddle. He had also brought some herbs as a poultice for Celia's wounds.

"I wouldn't have figured an army brat would know how to skin a rabbit," Davis said.

"I don't do it as well as Gerald, and my fingers are still a little stiff," Celia said, staring at the small animal in her hand, imitating Glidinghawk who was working by her side.

Compared to him, she was clumsy. He made one neat cut and peeled off the rabbit's fur like he was peeling off a glove. Still, she was managing.

"You are doing fine," Gerald told her.

"Even an officer's child learns a lot in the military

46

camps. If you didn't hunt, you could about starve on hardtack and fatback."

Celia hoped she sounded modest. Secretly, she was pleased by the comments of both men—and pleased that she had the opportunity to let them know she did a damned sight more than preside over kettledrums when she was growing up.

The fire had burned down to glowing embers, just right for roasting. The air was chill, but the smell of fresh coffee warmed Celia.

Aside from being flat out of booze—both she and Davis had found they enjoyed their evening ration—the night was perfect, crisp and clear under scattershot stars. Even without the whiskey, all three of them seemed uncommonly mellow.

They had weathered their first real crisis together. They had a reprieve before starting their mission in earnest. The stage only ran west two days a week. Gerald had scouted the area and found it clear of intruders.

The Indian added Celia's rabbit to the ones he had prepared, binding them to a green mesquite spit he had fashioned. He placed them over the coals. Soon, they were sputtering, dripping with juice.

Glidinghawk squatted on his haunches and stared at their feast. The smell made Celia's mouth water. She was thoroughly sick of the trail grub they had subsisted on. Salted bacon and beans was not her idea of good food.

Although, among them, Gerald was usually the most guarded, his past as closed as the masklike expression he habitually wore, he spoke now, breaking the pleasant silence.

"When I was at Dartmouth, I used to dream of meals

47

like this: fresh game sizzling over an open fire, under a sky so wide only the gods could cross it. Their idea of food was about as bad as the army's—put it in a pot and boil it until it looks, smells and tastes like it has been dead ten years. It was almost enough to make me want to turn cannibal. Maybe that's why my fellow students were afraid of the heathen."

Celia wrinkled up her nose. "I know. The food at Miss Parsons' was like that. It all tasted like oatmeal, even when it wasn't. And it all came out gray."

Glidinghawk laughed. Celia had never heard him laugh before, at least not a happy laugh. He did have a bitter sounding sarcastic bark that she had heard on several occasions, but this was very different. This sound was deep and musical, like clear water tumbling into a deep ravine.

"You know, I almost forgot you were sent to school only a couple hundred miles away from where I was . . . exiled," Glidinghawk said. "Do you ever wonder what we're doing out here—a young lady from finishing school and a Dartmouth graduate?"

Davis joined in with a chuckle. "I've led men before, but not with those qualifications. I know what I'm doing here . . . I think. But you, Celia? Why this?"

She was glad the flickering firelight hid her blushing cheeks. She recalled the pantywaist her aunt had wanted her to marry, only one minor reason she had fled westward. "I'll tell . . . if Gerald does."

For a moment, his Indian mask slipped down, closed and stony. But something in the night pushed it back, opening up what had been closed and guarded between them. "Ladies first," he said.

"All right," Celia agreed. She hoped she would not make herself sound silly. She spoke quickly. "Dime novels were my secret vice. I didn't want to end up as an old maid school teacher. So there."

Davis protested, "That's it? There must be more. Besides, you would be the last woman to end up as an old maid, with your looks."

"And my willful temper," Celia cut in. "Oh, you know what it's like, both in the army and back east. Those men want a woman who sits home all day, who always does the right thing . . . who embroiders doilies, for gawd's sake. And if I didn't want that, I didn't have many choices."

"Not too different from why I'm here," Gerald said, averting his face to check the rabbits. He took the two smaller ones off the spit and dumped them on tin plates as he talked.

"I didn't fit in the white man's world. My folks—the missionaries who raised me—thought I could. They wanted me to become a preacher. They didn't know that I'd have the white God kicked right out of me at school, but that's what happened."

"So?" Davis asked.

"I finally went back and found I no longer fit into the Indian's world, either. So here I am. I guess this is my own, personal No Man's Land."

"And you're bitter," Landrum stated dryly.

"And you're not? Celia's not? I don't think any of us would be here if we weren't," Glidinghawk said.

The glow had worn off the night. For a while, they ate in silence, each lost in his or her own thoughts.

Finally, Davis said, "Maybe you're right, Glidinghawk. I remember when I was little, back before the war, everything seemed sharper somehow. My folks were settlers, saw the first flag of Texas raised right after I was born. I grew up believing that I could carve an empire out of the land . . . but that was before a lot of things."

"And now? What are you getting out of this game—this working for the army?"

"Same as you," Landrum said, chuckling again. "Eight hundred dollars a year—and not in paper. And maybe, someday, a chance to buy a ranch, a chance to buy myself a slice of life the way I want to live it."

The mention of money reminded Celia of something she had wanted to ask. Besides, she didn't mind steering this conversation in a different direction. It was painting a picture she could not accept. Not yet, anyway. She wanted to think of them as heroes, not misfits.

"What happens to the money we make from our cover jobs? I expect they will pay me something for dealing cards, won't they?"

"Yes, and Landrum will be making a fortune out of buffalo hides," Gerald said.

"Well, you'll be making something, too," Celia reminded him.

"As an outcast Indian swamper in a saloon?" Gerald said acidly. "I'll be lucky if they throw me a counterfeit coin now and then."

Davis raised his hand to quiet them. "Any extra money we make is ours, at least that's the way I figure it. I admit I hadn't thought about the two of us making a bundle while Glidinghawk . . . aw hell! If life was fair, we wouldn't be here, would we? Let's just make it through this mission alive, and we'll see what happens."

They chewed on that along with the roasted rabbit.

Like the shooting of the night before, this was the way it had to be. Period. Celia was finding that a lot out here was like that. Black and white. You survived. You could not afford to question.

Although she had spent part of her growing years in the West, she had never fully understood before how wild and untamed the land was—as were the men who would tame it. But looking up at the broad sky blanketed with stars, she felt its glory and freedom, too. For the first time in many years, she felt that she belonged.

In the distance, an owl hooted. Gerald listened as if his ear were catching every vibration carried on the wind, and shook his head. It was only an owl.

Davis stood up and stretched. "One more day," he said. "I want to go over everything in the morning, again and again, until we all have it right. No more bumbling disasters."

Before they bedded down for the night, Gerald looked at Celia's hands again. "The lacerations probably feel worse than they are," he said. "If you can skin a rabbit with these hands, you'll be able to deal a wicked game of faro."

"Don't remind me," Celia said. "I want to sleep tonight. I don't want to think about Fort Griffin."

Gerald rubbed her fingers with the same salve he had used earlier. It smelled like old socks, though slightly medicinal, and looked twice as rank.

His touch was comforting. An energy seemed to flow from his competent, bronzed hands to her smaller white ones. "The Omaha have a saying . . . it's not too different from things I have heard the white man say."

"What is it?" Celia asked.

"Let the day's troubles be sufficient unto the day, because. . . ." Gerald's voice drifted off.

"What?" Celia whispered solemnly.

"All the rest is buffalo chips."

Only Davis, standing alone in the shadows, did not laugh. He skittered a stone with his boot as he averted his brooding eyes.

CHAPTER FIVE

Davis had been right. Catching the stage had been as easy as a pig sliding into a wallow. Glidinghawk rode into the deserted stage outpost from camp in the early morning hours.

By sunup, Celia seemed to have magically appeared—the mysterious lady gambler extending her gloved hand for a ticket. A whiskered buckboard driver, reeking of pure grain alcohol, accepted her money and motioned to an equally sotted lasher, who tossed her carpetbag atop the mail sacks.

A fellow passenger eyed her curiously, but he no more would have asked her where she came from than he would ask a man for his real name. Instead, he leered with blackened teeth.

Celia's spirits soared briefly—until the small stage lurched onward with teeth-chattering monotony, slowly covering the distance to Fort Griffin. She was glad they had only seven miles to go. It would be, she realized, a long seven miles.

The man opposite her definitely looked like a dolt—homespun, bulging cheeks of a tobacco addict, hair like down and the richocheting eyes of a chicken. Celia did not want to encourage his friendship.

She pretended to have an interest in the landscape, but after the majesty of the sweeping plains with its waist-high grasses sighing in the wind, this scrubland looked as barren and cratered as a fanciful illustration she had once seen of the moon.

The man beside her shot a wad of brown juice out the window. The wind spit back hissing drops, scorning his offering. Celia shuddered.

"Didn't 'spect no woman," the man shrugged, as if it was her tough luck. He reached for a fresh plug.

It was the high point of conviviality for the trip.

Celia was not overly impressed by Ben Ficklin's Stage and Mail Line.

They slewed into a turn by the Clear Fork of the Brazos. Directly ahead loomed the Flats, a ragtag collection of clapboard and false fronts as unreal and insubstantial as an obscene child's toy town, brand new but broken by Christmas revelry.

One by one, as day met dusk, the lights of saloons sparkled on with nocturnal promise. Soldiers on pass milled in the streets, jostling one another. As Celia disembarked, a young enlisted man caterwauled a welcome as he caught sight of her petticoat flapping like a white flag.

Celia accepted her heavy bag from the lasher and surveyed the scene. About five hundred yards away was the planked barricade of the fort itself. That—and the whooping soldiers freed for the night—gave her a sense of familiarity. As she dimly recalled her mother saying, "If you've seen one army post, you've seen them all."

Only, as her intelligent green eyes took in the crib-lined alleys and rutted streets, glittering brighter as night closed in, Celia realized she must have been shielded from some of life's realities.

The denizens of Texas Street in Abilene paled beside the number of fallen women who were boldly parading their buxom wares—perhaps because Marshal Hickok had cleaned up that cattle town, although Celia had found it far from lily white.

Here, she saw an exchange between a street woman and a reeling man in uniform. The heavy-bosomed woman darted in front of him, stopping him cold. She forced his calloused hand to her bared upper breast. Mercifully, they strolled away before continuing their amorous grappling.

Celia sniffed. She was not a prude, but she hoped no one would mistake her for . . . one of them. Her long hair was piled on top of her head, securely fastened with pins. Her traveling suit was demure, she thought, without inviting attention to her anatomy.

However, she was anxious to find shelter. A strong arm grabbed her elbow from behind. Her heart fluttered up in her throat like a flock of quail. She turned, ready to swing.

"Whoa! I thought you might need some help with your carpetbag. Are you one of Madam Agnes' new girls?"

Tall, limber, black tailcoat and ruffled stark white shirt setting off a smooth-planed face, his facade inspired confidence. His words did not.

"I am not a fancy lady!" Celia snorted.

"My apologies. For a moment, I thought you were assaying the competition. In any case, may I be of service? They call me Jack. Black Jack."

"A gambling man?" Celia asked.

"Is there any other kind?"

"Not as far as I am concerned," Celia told him, stifling the tremor in her throat. "I am a faro dealer myself, looking for work. But first, I will need to secure a room. If you could tell me of a respectable boarding house, I would be most grateful."

The polite phrases that had been drummed into her had a way of sounding much different—highly suggestive, in fact—out here. She could tell the question of how grateful was in his mind, if not on his lips.

When he stifled it, Celia truly was grateful.

"No place in the Flats is exactly respectable, but the hotel up the street comes as close as any. I stay there myself, as do other members of the gambling circuit. Maybe you'll run into some old friends."

Circuit? Old friends?

She let it ride as they neared the Vagabond Hotel. A new sign with curling serifs declared it to be Fort Griffin's finest, but it already looked shabby.

The hotel clerk looked like the twin of the one at Drovers' Cottage. Celia wondered if Western hotels attracted officious mice, rather than men, to gnaw at their front desks. This one appeared to know Black Jack.

"A room for the lady," Jack said. He stressed the word *lady*.

The clerk nodded and handed Black Jack a key, giving him a sly grin. "Is this by the hour, the night or the week?"

"I have never heard of renting a room by the hour," Celia declared in a huff. Then she colored. "By the week," she snapped.

She signed the register and turned pointedly to the tall

dandy by her side. "And my thanks to you, Mr. Black Jack, for carrying my bags. Perhaps we shall meet again."

"I was hoping so," he said lazily, slate gray eyes flickering with amusement. "I would be glad to introduce you to the gambling establishments here. Say, in an hour?"

The bottom seemed to fall out of Celia's stomach as she accepted. To make a date with an unknown man—to be totally free of chaperones at night in a wicked city—was beyond her experience. She had longed for this freedom, and now that it was here she felt like she was sailing into a pit that had no bottom.

Celia insisted on a hot bath and made do with a basin of water. At least it was clear. She sponged off her traveling suit, decided it was not daring enough, and finally settled for a broadcloth gown with a scooped neck. It showed just a hint of cleavage.

She secured her derringer in her garter.

She was waiting in the lobby with ten minutes to spare. The shot of adrenaline spurred by actually being here had wiped away her fatigue. Besides, she reminded herself, she would have to get used to late hours.

Black Jack was late. She paced. The clerk coughed irritably. A rotund medicine drummer, with his arm around a fleshy woman, hired a room for an hour. The clerk hrumphed significantly. Celia decided, not for the first time, that she disliked hotel clerks.

At last Black Jack arrived, and the rest of the night swirled by in an explosion of color and glitter. He was a dashing escort. He knew all the places and, at each, they knew him. They accorded him the respect of a successful gambling man.

The Northern, The Bull's Tail (as opposed, Celia's rum-swimming head told her, to the animal's head), The Lone Star, The Cavalry Club, Lotte Deno's Poker Den, and the newest and liveliest of them all, the Brazos Club.

Celia's biggest mistake, she would realize the next morning, was the first shot of whiskey on an almost empty stomach. But instead of making her slow or sleepy, it burned right through her like a new life.

She flirted with the men—she met so many that she could not remember their names. She batted her eyelashes at Jack, who took her arm when she faltered and showed her around like a prize pig at a fair. At the time, it seemed only a token of his admiration.

She tried out the faro tables, fingers flying with chips, daring the house to take her money. It was a lucky night, or the dealers were entranced by the glowing redhead. She won. Laughter burst out of her like it came from a deep well that had never been tapped before.

Celia could never remember having so much fun. She was on top of the world. Scores of honky-tonk owners invited her to work for them. She giggled and said she would see tomorrow, because tomorrow seemed like forever away.

Tonight, she was the greatest thespian that ever lived. She was no longer Celia Louise Burnett, just Celia, gambling lady freed of the past and future, out for a night on the town. And she had already found her handsome, valiant protector.

It was all wonderful . . . until Black Jack nodded to some cronies of his, men with avid eyes sitting around a poker table at The Golden Mount, and his slate eyes turned restless.

"I think you've had enough," he said. "I'm taking you back to the hotel." He turned to the cardsharps. "Later, gentlemen."

The change in him quieted her. Had her last words been too loud, verging on hysteria? Did he think she was—it pained her to even think the word—drunk?

Speaking clearly and carefully, she said, "I had a very long day. If you would be so kind, I would like to call it a night. If you please?"

He hooked her arm in his and they strolled through the streets, deserted except for a few stragglers. The night was being eaten away by a gradual lightening of the sky. The air, chill in the early morning hours of April, sobered Celia, but she accepted his help upstairs.

At her door, his hands tipped her chin up to meet his. She had never been kissed like this before. It sent a flood of warmth through her.

"I might take advantage of a man at a card table who has imbibed too much," he said in a hoarse whisper, "but I wouldn't do that to you, Celia."

She felt like screaming. She wanted to hold on to him. Instead, she said, "Thank you."

"Because you know something, young lady? You have a lot of gumption, but you aren't quite as worldly as you pretend to be. And I'm not sure you would still like me in the morning."

"Will I see you again?"

"Tomorrow," he promised.

Celia felt an emptiness when he turned his broad shoulders and descended the staircase. As she fitted her key in the lock, she realized she had been awake for over twenty-four hours. Everything hit her all at once with the impact of slashing hail.

She did not know why she cried, but she did, alone in the hotel room, with apparitions of Landrum and Gerald and Black Jack and her dead father appearing just out of focus, just out of reach.

At last, she slept. She dreamed of the contained green of a faro layout, and hands reaching out to copper a bet on the queen.

CHAPTER SIX

"Nice hands," saloon owner Samuel Wallace said, placing one of his hairy hands over Celia's and squeezing as if he were testing the ripeness of a summer melon. His palms were damp and oily. "I want to see them raking in the chips tonight."

Celia drew away as he forced her right-hand palm upward. He stared at the faint scars, which had healed to a pink as smooth as a baby's toothless gums. Whatever Glidinghawk had used to doctor them had worked quickly.

Celia smiled a green little smile at Samuel and flexed her fingers against the dealing box beside the faro layout. Something about the man pawing her sent shivers up her spine. His balding pate, waxed handlebar mustache and pear-shaped paunch beneath a brocade vest made him look like an aging fop.

The greasiness of his collar, the sallowness of his waxy skin and the beadiness of his lecherous eyes made the closeup view even less attractive. And his name was Sam, the same as the horse thief that Glidinghawk had killed. The association was not comforting.

Neither was the frown that Madam Agnes shot across

the room like a venomous arrow. Somehow, the Brazos Club had seemed like a much friendlier place last night, when she had been a guest escorted by Black Jack. Tonight, she was an employee—or would be, officially, if everything went well.

Samuel also noticed the plump madam's angry eyes, and he hastily backed off. "The real crowd won't be in for a couple hours. Today was payday out at the fort, so you'll have plenty of action. Stack the deck with as many pairs as you can, and take them for all you can get."

Celia bit her lip. She knew, of course, that most games of faro were crooked. Stacking pairs was the most common way of cheating—the house automatically raked off half the bet.

People expected to get stung when they bucked the tiger. It did not prevent men from being drawn to the game like flies to honey.

"I expect your table will be packed," Samuel said, turning to leave. "Besides the cavalry, the hiders will be in, and they have more money. Sweet talk them. They might smell like buffalo innards, but they've got the gold."

"I'll do my best," Celia said, shifting her feet. Already, they hurt. Standing here all night would be a feat of endurance. She could tell that dealing for fun—as she had always done—and dealing for a living were two very different things.

"You do that," Samuel said. "I'm assigning Sneaky Pete as your casekeeper, and Farley as your lookout. They'll keep an eye on both you and the customers. You do good tonight, and you got a steady job here."

He nodded to the men in rolled up shirtsleeves and suspenders who strolled over to her faro bank. Pete, the younger one, would work the abacuslike device that kept track of the cards already dealt. Farley, the one with a face like a bear, would watch both Celia and the crowd.

The way faro was played, there were thirteen replica cards on Celia's board, each one representing a number or face card. Suits did not count. The bettors would place their chips on the board cards, as many as twenty bettors crowding around the same table.

Celia would deal from the spring-action box that held the deck, pulling out cards from "soda" to "hock," first card to last. The first card, or soda, was a dead card. After that, every two cards represented a turn. The card placed over the soda was a loser, the second card exposed face up in the dealing box was the winner—unless the bettor had placed another marker over his bet, coppering it, betting it to lose. The game flew along, twenty-five turns to a deck.

Farley, a giant of a man, took a stand beside Celia, eyeing her bosom with evident interest. He sucked on a bad tooth. Celia felt self-conscious. Samuel Wallace had ordered her to expose as much of her cleavage as possible.

She had worn the same dress as last night, only she had minimized some of the bodice fabric by pleating it with her brooch. She was not used to the cool air against such an expanse of bared skin.

"Nice," Farley grunted.

Sneaky Pete, taking his position beside Celia, nodded in agreement. He was a cherubic blond with pudgy fingers and the soul of a petty swindler. "You good at this?" he asked her.

Celia was not about to tell him that she had learned faro as a parlor game and had never worked as a professional. She knew her hands were quick. She knew some of the tricks, like stacking the deck. She hoped she would pass. "Fair," she said. "A little out of practice."

Pete nodded. He was not too happy. He liked to deal himself and now he would be second fiddle. Still, a woman had a chance of making a bundle for their bank, and he and Farley planned to split part of it.

"Just keep calling the turns real fast and we'll take care of the rest," he told her.

She hadn't been set up ten minutes when the first bettors appeared. By the time she fumbled through the first deck, the action was so swift that Celia did not have time to worry about how well she was doing.

Her whole world was reduced to thirteen squares and fifty-two cards turning over and over in an endless round. Chips chunked and clicked across the board, most raked off for the house.

The Brazos Club was relatively new and surprisingly fancy. Diagonally across from the Bee Hive, another gambling den, dance hall and saloon, it tried to outdo its neighbor. Cut-glass chandeliers, a polished oak bar over forty feet long and a small string band gave it a veneer of civilization.

The fancy-dressed women who worked for Madam Agnes and the reclining, Renaissance-style nudes on the walls completed the tawdry splendor. Celia outshone all but one of the high-class calico queens, a statuesque blond with ample bosoms and a smile as generous as her curvaceous hips.

Her name, Celia had learned, was Nellie Vernon, or at least that was the name she used. She was regal, dressed in satin, not calico, and as alluring as any woman Celia had ever laid eyes on.

Though easily the most popular of Madam Agnes' girls,

Nellie appeared very selective about who would accompany her to her room. According to rumor, Nellie conducted her business in the frilliest French undergarments, and only those with particularly large sums of money had ever been allowed to explore the incredible mounds of her womanflesh. Those who had experienced the pleasure were never the same, adding credence to the belief that a night of passion with Nellie Vernon could drive a man mad.

But Nellie was an exception. The common frontier prostitute, Celia had found, had looks that owed more to the inebriation and deprivation of her customer than to any standard of beauty.

"Last turn," Celia sang out, briefly eyeing the men tossing away their money as her fingers flipped cards. "Anyone want to call it?"

A young soldier with a peach-fuzz mustache had lost most of his paycheck. Celia felt sorry for him. He was too young—probably younger than she was—for this life.

He looked as innocent as a lamb to the slaughter. She turned her eyes back to the cards and the layout, empty now of chips.

"I'll call," the young soldier announced, eagerly extending his last chips like a sacrifice.

The friend who had been watching him lose, groaned, "Aw, Homer, you won't have nothing left for the pigpens."

"You want to bet?" Homer said. He checked the casekeeper to see which cards had yet to be played. "I call the ten, the ace and the five."

It was an almost sure bet for the house, though it paid four to one in the unlikely event someone could call it. Odds against naming the last two cards and the hock in sequence were against all but the most canny bettor.

Celia had been dealing by rote, without paying too much attention. She was resigned that the game was crooked as the night would be long. Now, she perked up as a ten slid out of the dealing box first.

As the second card was revealed—an ace—a collective intake of breath hissed through the air. Celia's table was the first one of the evening to fill up. Men stood around watching the play and teasing Celia. They called her Red. The spunky redhead was already a great attraction.

Everyone knew the hock would be the five, but it was not until it was laid out that Homer yelped, "Whoopie!"

Celia smiled at him as she paid out. It was her first genuine smile of the night, and it lit up her face. It was a mistake. Madam Agnes saw the commotion from her perch at the bar and frowned, her thick, dark eyebrows drawing together like slinky black snakes.

"Co'mon, Homer," the soldier's friend pleaded plaintively, "let's get out of here while you have something left."

Celia started the new game. She saw Homer hesitate, itching to buck the tiger again. His friend pounded him on the arm. Homer's eyes were spinning keno pellets as he wavered, undecided. Celia could almost read his thoughts: whiskey, women or more gambling? She was glad when he turned away, though why, she didn't know. He would only throw away his money somewhere else. She could not feel responsible for every sucker that played at her table. Still, she felt good when he left, looking back at her as if she had been Lady Luck herself dealing kindly with him.

As the tempo of the night picked up, Celia could no longer keep the faces of strangers straight. Soldiers in uniform breathing fresh whiskey in her face, Sneaky Pete with fingers flying to keep up with the cards, Farley grunting from time to time—these impressions dimly registered.

Cards. Celia had loved dealing since she was a girl. They sang to her, slipping from her nimble hands, soda to hock, hour after hour. The saloon had filled up with merrymakers. She was wrapped up in her work, but from time to time, in the seconds between deals, she looked to the bar, hoping to see the smooth-planed face of Black Jack.

She saw the wide shoulders of a man dressed in black and her heart leapt, but when he turned his head, his face was pocked and mean and one she had never seen before.

Samuel Wallace had been right about the buffalo hunters, Celia realized as her nose wrinkled at the stench that mixed badly with the whiskey fumes. All day her stomach had been queasy, and it was no help remembering what a tipsy fool she had made of herself last night.

It had been a very odd day, what was left of it when she had finally woken up. It had not taken her long to learn that the last man who was murdered in the Falts had been with Nellie Vernon the last time he had been seen.

The victim's name was Seth Downey, and he had been a striker—personal houseboy—for a Major Newcomb at the fort.

At the cafe where Celia had ordered a late lunch of buffalo steak, they had told her about the body, about how it had been found in an alley, disemboweled. The woman who owned the cafe recited the gory details with relish.

That, and the after-effects of her night on the town, had set Celia off food. But she had learned that Nellie was

Madam Agnes' top girl, and Madam Agnes operated out of Samuel Wallace's new club.

From there, it had been easy. Samuel was delighted, he said with a drop of spittle settling on the tip of his handlebar, to have her work for him. Lady gamblers were rare and treasured. He beamed and pawed, until Madam Agnes called out to him in a strident voice.

Celia had waited at a table, listening to his low voice and the woman's higher, shriller one arguing in the back room. When Samuel returned, his liverish lips were set in a grim line, but he said, "We will try you out." He made it clear that even a lady gambler needed to prove her worth. He also made it clear that he and the madam had different opinions on the subject of Celia.

As the memory faded, Celia cleared her board. Not a single customer had won that turn and she knew she was doing well enough to assure her employment on a more permanent basis. She saw a pair of hands plunk a chip down on the queen, hesitate, and move it to the jack. The hands looked tough and strong and familiar.

She looked up and immediately dropped her eyes, hoping the fringe of her lashes would hide the light of recognition. Landrum Davis had elbowed his way through the throng and stood there, another bettor, another sucker.

Landrum's buckskins were cleaner than those of the other hiders and he was taller than she remembered. She wished she could talk to him and tell him what she had learned, but she could tell from his easy stance that he did not need to speak to her. He had only been trying to get her attention.

"A lady dealer," he said approvingly, an innocuous comment that told Celia he was pleased with how well she was playing her role.

"And a sharp one, too," another man grumbled without animosity. "This little gal has about cleaned me out."

"What's her name?" Landrum asked, addressing Farley who was staring, bored, at the play.

"Red," the lookout answered in a surly tone. "Place your bet and quit gawking, hider."

Landrum lost a few chips—enough so Celia knew he was there, knew he was watching out for her—and sidled away toward the bar. He ordered a shot of whiskey and ogled Nellie Vernon. All part of the job, Celia reminded herself, but she felt a twinge of irritation.

Her feet hurt like Hades now, and she wondered how long it would be until she could take a break. The rhythm of the cards was losing its thrall. What had glittered last night now palled. She had never imagined that dealing round after round of faro could become boring.

The faces in front of her, soldiers and hiders and a few cowboys, all began to look the same. Thin faces, fat faces, hairy ones and clean-shaven ones, all possessing gambler's eyes—that intense concentration on the cards, that clicking of eyelids like the clicking of chips. Win or lose. Win or lose. . . .

"Disgraceful!"

A pompous voice broke the rhythm. It belonged to a soldier in dress uniform bearing the stripes of a second lieutenant. The smug, smooth face, presently turned down in lines of disapproval, was not particularly memorable. It was the kind of face that you feel you have seen before, but can't remember and, frankly, don't really care to.

Except Celia suddenly did remember, and the memory made her lose her composure for the first time since beginning work. The name Preston Kirk Fox charged into her head along with the image of everything Celia had always hated about the army.

The damned fool seemed strained in his efforts to cover the fact that he knew her.

"Do you want to place a bet, sir?" she asked sharply.

Farley moved into position behind the rude soldier, sensing trouble. Farley had fists the size and texture of smoked hams, and he raised them now, ready to pull the troublemaker away from Celia's table.

"Oh, all right!" Fox huffed, placing a chip on the six. Celia dealt. The six, when it came up, was a losing number.

Fox insinuated himself into the middle of the big bettors who were tossing their money out like they were anxious to part with it. He placed single bets at stingy intervals, all the while gulping and popping his eyes out like a fly-catching frog.

It was disconcerting. The man was trying to say something, and Celia found herself watching his facial gymnastics with real horror.

Fox mumbled, "A woman working in a honky-tonk like this . . . along with the whores . . . this is not to be countenanced."

The disparaging muttering was getting on Celia's nerves. At any second, the fool could blow her cover. As covertly as she could manage in her near-panic, she swept the room with her eyes.

She saw Landrum striding over to her table. He had seen Fox. Stepping forward, he dug an elbow into the younger man's ribs, causing Fox to exhale sharply as he was forced out of the way. Landrum then scattered chips across the board, as if he had been away from the faro bank too long and was hot to play.

Fox glared at him and loudly announced, "It is immoral for this woman to be dealing cards in a whorehouse."

A hush opened up like a fan around them.

The first violin of the string band wheezed to a halt. Hundreds of eyes stared at the tall, lean hider turned to glare at the dapper soldier. Their fellow bettors formed a ring around them.

"Soldier boy," Landrum said calmly, "we like a woman dealer just fine. You think different, you take your business elsewhere."

Lieutenant Fox started to say something that sounded like, "I will report this to—"

But he never finished.

Landrum let loose with an uppercut to the jaw and Fox dropped to the floor. His head made a sickening plop against the floorboards.

From the bar, a calico queen shrieked. The band resumed playing with a sound like chalk on a blackboard before picking up the tune they had halted in mid-note.

Celia shivered in relief.

Farley dragged the unconscious soldier off toward the front entrance, but Madam Agnes stopped him. "This soldier is in tight with the major," she rasped. "Put him in the upstairs bedroom."

A humming buzz of knockout post mortems swelled the air. As Landrum returned to her side, Celia tossed her head back and said brazenly, "Thank you, hider. Now,

71

let's all buck the tiger!"

After that, Celia's table was jammed, the men three deep around her. She did not notice when Landrum slipped away. Nor was she aware that Madam Agnes was staring over at her with a mixture of greed and suspicion. And more than a touch of envy.

CHAPTER SEVEN

In the early morning hours, business slackened off.

Shifts changed. Another dealer came to take Celia's place. She finished out her deal, scooped up the chips that had not already been collected, and handed them to Farley.

As lookout, the chips were Farley's responsibility. Throughout the night, he had run them over to Samuel on an hourly basis for tallying.

Farley and Sneaky Pete wasted no time getting away from the table, now that their shifts were through. Celia followed the short casekeeper, tottering over to the bar where the other dealers were gathering.

"A shot," a dealer called Lucky Jim ordered.

"God, yes," said another. "Payday at the fort calls for libation."

The barkeeper thumped a bottle of Squirrel and a brace of glasses across the counter. "S'right," he agreed.

"This snake piss again?" Sneaky Pete groaned.

"Complain to the boss," the bartender said.

Celia could tell it was a nightly ritual. Lucky Jim took the amber bottle over to a round table. The others sat themselves there, and Celia joined them, sinking into the chair and wriggling her numb feet.

"You get yourself some better shoes," Lucky Jim advised, sliding glasses across the tabletop with the same practiced ease with which he dealt cards. "I recall when I was a young dealer—it was the feet that did me in."

Another dealer grunted in assent and began an involved story about a man known as Barefoot Bob, who used to slip his boots off before beginning his night's work. Unfortunately, his boss discovered that he slipped a cache of chips into his empty boots. One night, the boss hid a small snake in Barefoot Bob's boot. According to the legend, the crooked dealer became known as Honest Bob.

Seven dealers, including Celia, four casekeepers and an equal number of lookouts eventually gathered at the table. With the heavy concentration of the night finally put behind them, they could relax. Some of the men, like Jim, topped their shots with beer.

Celia's throat was dry. She asked for a beer and skipped the shot. It was unladylike to drink beer, but it tasted cool and good. She could tell that she would have to be careful. Drinking could get to be a bad habit.

Out on the floor, the graveyard shift had been reduced to three active tables, and the string band had packed it in an hour earlier.

The few women who had not drummed up some business earlier sat at a separate table, still hoping. Celia recognized the fleshy one as Big Lil, and the one with dark skin as Colored Susan, but she could not remember the names of the others, or if she had even been told.

The dealers' talk was pleasant, full of barroom gossip. Pete got out a deck of cards and challenged all comers, but no one took him up on a game. Instead, Lucky Jim said, "Not now. I have half a mind to trot over to the Golden Mount and see how the big poker game is going."

"Hear they's playing up a storm."

"The way they was going wild, I reckon almost $20,000 was riding on the hand they was playing around midnight," Farley said.

"Who's left in the game?"

"The Major, that banker Phillip Kiley, some hider name of Deitz and Black Jack. They was raisin' last time I heard."

So that's where Black Jack is, Celia thought. She had been disappointed that he had not shown up. Now she understood why. Perhaps that was why he left last night and not, as Celia had feared all day, because she had had too much to drink. She wondered how any human being could keep going for days, playing poker.

She listened to some of her cohorts make plans for the rest of the night. She was amazed. Most planned to hit a few different saloons before sleeping. Days and nights were jumbled up, almost reversed, for the people who worked the honky-tonks.

Having been accepted by the other dealers, Celia took a moment to appreciate her role. It was rather nice, sitting around the table with work done, while Samuel counted the money in the back room. Celia had never had so much money pass through her hands in one night. Even so, $20,000 riding on Black Jack's poker game still seemed unreal.

Samuel stepped out from the back room and a hush fell on the relaxed conversation. "Lucky Jim, your bank is short tonight," he said.

The mutton-chopped gambler shrugged. "You got yourself a hot dealer with Red here," he said, pointing to

Celia, "and it's bound to tell on our tallies."

Another faro dealer agreed. "That's right, Sam. Even my regulars deserted. Don't seem fair they'd as soon lose money to a smiling woman. Aren't we pretty enough for them?"

Laughter broke the tension, but Samuel said, "I guess you're right, but next time, Farley's going to be your lookout, Jim."

"I don't take kindly to that," Lucky Jim said.

"Then you find yourself another place that'll treat you as good as we do," Sam said.

"I might just do that," the dealer said.

"Celia . . . I guess I should call you Red . . . I want to see you in my office," Samuel announced.

Reluctantly, she slipped her pointed-toe shoes back on her swollen feet and followed. The back room was little more than a cubicle with a desk and some straight-back chairs.

The glamor of the Brazos Club ended at the great divide. Areas denied access to paying customers were unfinished board and strictly business. If chips and gold coins could have been counted on a planked table, that's what would have been there.

One side of the little office led to another, larger room where cases of booze were stored. It was a pernicious arrangement, designed to keep a close watch on the stock. Celia could tell that the opulence of the club was an illusion; Samuel Wallace accounted for every penny his joint took in like the stingiest of shopkeepers.

She took the chair he indicated, surprised when he extracted a bottle of French brandy and two shot glasses from his desk drawer. "Private stock," he told her.

She accepted, not so much from a desire to drink as to

have something to do with her hands. She hoped this interview would not take long. She knew she had circles under her eyes from fatigue.

"You did all right," Samuel said in what Celia felt was an intentional understatement. He twisted the ends of the mustache that almost made up for the lack of hair on his head. "Yes, you and me can do all right. . . ."

His nose quivered, making his moustache twitch in response. His eyes bulged slightly. Celia stifled an urge to giggle as he lifted his arms, reaching toward her. *He looks like a rabbit in heat,* Celia thought, bringing her glass to the lips that threatened to reveal her amusement. She took a slug of her drink.

When her face was straight and controlled again, she asked, "That means I have a steady job here?"

A lumbering step sounded behind her. She saw Sam's hands—those same sweaty hands she had endured earlier—retreat quickly to his side of the desk.

"Well, well," Madam Agnes demanded, her whiskey voice strident. "How cozy. And with my private stock."

Samuel grinned sheepishly. "Thought the girl deserved it. She is going to make us all a lot of money."

Agnes leaned across the desk and grabbed the brandy bottle. Sam hastily clanked another glass out and she poured herself a shot. "Could be," Agnes said. "I've seen better dealers. You could have stacked more pairs and kept the bets moving faster."

Celia was peering at the madam's ample hips, which were in a direct line with her green eyes. The madam's green satin dress sighed and strained at the seams. Closeup, like Samuel, Madam Agnes' glitter lacked freshness. Her perfume overlay a sour smell.

"I'm sure I can do better tomorrow," Celia said.

Agnes tilted her glass back and swallowed with a shuddering quiver of flesh. She leaned back, hipshod against the desk, giving Samuel the view of her spreading derriere. She stared at Celia critically.

"I told Samuel we'd try you." Her grimace revealed gold teeth. "But as much as I like making money, I don't want no trouble with any of my women, including you. Did you know that soldier from somewhere? He know you?"

Celia had been afraid the scene with Fox would be brought to her attention. She had dreaded it. Her voice was flat when she said, "I don't have any husbands or former lovers chasing me down if that's what you are asking. The man was drunk and out of line. That was not my fault."

"Maybe not," Madam Agnes said. "I don't ask for a woman's real name or where she's from, but all my girls fit here. You . . . ," Agnes paused as if choosing her words carefully. Or maybe it was just that words—any words—had become lost somewhere between the madam's mind and mouth, Celia thought.

"Just look at that dress," she finally said. "Why, you could practically wear it to church. We don't want no proper ladies."

"I was hired to deal faro, not flesh," Celia said sharply, and immediately regretted it. If the madam threw her out, she'd have to start looking for another cover, setting the investigation back at least another day.

"She's right, Agnes," Samuel said in Celia's defense. "You run your girls and I run the tables."

"I will tell you what you run and how you run it."

Samuel's sallow skin flushed, but he kept his mouth shut. The silence stretched out. Finally, Madam Agnes

78

asked what the take on Celia's table had been. She flashed her gold teeth at the tally.

Agnes patted Celia on the shoulder, her hostility replaced by greed. "This could work out all right. I saw those men looking at you. If you ever change your mind about being just a dealer, you let me know," Madam Agnes brayed. "I don't want trouble with soldiers, like tonight. And you find yourself a better dressmaker. Give the boys a gander of the merchandise, even if they can't touch. Could be good for business all around. Maybe Sam's right about you. Maybe a woman can make as much on her feet as on her back."

The employees' table had broken up.

Celia was relieved. The bartender motioned to her, and showed her a side door she could use, so that she didn't have to face any all-night revelers on her way out. She reached down and checked on her derringer. On second thought, she extracted it from her garter and hid it in her shawl; it would be handy if she encountered trouble.

The Vagabond Hotel was three blocks away, down rutted streets, past alleys lined with cribs. The women who worked there were the dregs of their profession. Looking from the darkness, Celia could see the cots and washbasins inside—and the half-naked woman, waiting.

Pigpens. The name fit. Their ramshackled huts looked like places fit only for hogs. Involuntarily, Celia shuddered. It was a long fall from the saloons and high class places like the Brazos Club to the tiny cubicles built for only one thing—and it was not gracious living.

A group of three men wove their way up the street. Celia ducked into a shadow, but one of them saw her. He grabbed for her. She grabbed for her derringer, as a shabby Indian roiled out and crashed into the man, knocking him sideways.

"Damnation!" the man cursed, struggling to regain his balance. By the time his friends had helped steady him, the lone Indian had disappeared and Celia was scurrying up the street, rushing into the lobby of the hotel.

She got her key from the clerk and trudged up the stairs, her feet aching. Through the thin hotel walls, she heard grunts and sighs and the creaking of bed springs.

She locked the door behind her, tossed her shawl and gun on the bedside table, and kicked off her shoes. Then she shrugged out of her dress and sank back on the narrow cot, unfastening her corset stays with grunts and sighs of her own.

Suddenly, the hair at the nape of her neck bristled. Her heart thudded in her ears. She had locked herself in—along with the someone else she was suddenly aware of. There was no sound or movement, only the feeling of another person nearby. Fear paralyzed her.

She sensed the presence hiding near the wardrobe. Whalebone bit into her tender breast flesh as she twisted around and reached for the gun she had carelessly tossed aside.

"Don't shoot," a familiar voice whispered urgently.

"Glidinghawk?"

"None other," Gerald said, stepping out with his arms raised. Then he gave her a mock bow. "At your service."

"Next time I'll shoot," Celia said, pulling her shawl up over her exposed breasts. "You could have let me know before I disrobed."

"You white women call that undressed?" Glidinghawk said. "You still have on layers and layers of clothing. And you don't have anything I haven't seen before."

Celia realized that she was being childish, but she was still embarrassed and angry at being caught like this. "What do you want?" she demanded.

Glidinghawk grinned. "It's what you want," he said. "Information."

Celia listened as he explained what he had picked up in the Flats. "Madam Agnes and Samuel Wallace are man and wife, though they don't advertise it. The madam is the brains behind their operation."

"I had that figured out," Celia said.

"Then you know about Nellie Vernon?"

"Some," Celia said. "The last man who was murdered bought her favors for the night. She was the last one to see him alive, as far as anyone knows. She claimed he paid for an hour and left after his time was up."

"Yes, like the others. Seth Downey was the third man to be murdered, and all were killed after buying the favors of Nellie Vernon."

"You don't think she could have murdered them?" Celia asked.

"No," Glidinghawk said. "There was too much force used. A woman could not have slashed them like that. But there is some connection. Maybe you can find out more from that fancy man of yours. . . ."

Celia started to protest, but Glidinghawk stopped her. "You didn't think Landrum and I would find out about last night? In fact, Landrum has a message for you, too. Lay off the firewater."

Heat sped to Celia's face. "What right does he have. . . ?"

Glidinghawk cut her off with a quick motion of his hand. "Don't get so loud. We said we would be watching out for you, and we are. You want to use the gambler for information—or anything else—that's fine. Just keep your head on your shoulders."

Celia bowed her head. He was right, of course. Her actions last night had not been in control. But it was the idea that she was being spied on, by her own team, that angered and embarrassed her. She wondered if Glidinghawk had seen the passionate kiss Black Jack had given her—and she had returned with equal fervor.

"You could pick worse for a companion," Glidinghawk mused, "as far as the mission goes. And as long as you work him, instead of the other way around."

For the second time that night Celia was about to protest that she was not a prostitute, when she stopped herself. She was supposed to be a gambling woman and gambling women had liaisons. In fact, the idea appealed to her almost as much as it scared her.

"Gerald, you tell me to get close to Nellie, and . . . well, get friendly with Black Jack. But what if they find out that I never . . . that I'm a . . . ," she paused, unable to bring herself to spit out the word.

". . . that you're a virgin?" Glidinghawk asked. Celia's cheeks flamed as she watched Gerald twitch, straining to maintain control of himself. "It never occurred to me . . ." Glidinghawk began, pausing to clear his throat before continuing. "That is, I can't imagine Lieutenant Colonel Amos Powell asking you in your interview—"

"I knew it," Celia wailed, inferring from Gerald's reaction that he was making fun of her. "Damn you. It isn't funny."

"The condition itself, no," Glidinghawk said, breaking into a grin. "But you have to admit, the situation is amusing. If it concerns you that much, I would be willing

82

to assist in any way I can."

"I'll bet you would," Celia hissed. "How long has it been since you've had a white woman, Injun?"

Gerald whirled away as if he had been slapped. At last, he said, "Then it is your problem. I've passed on the information Landrum thought you should have. What you do with it is your business."

He turned and slipped out the back window of Celia's room. She stared after him, stunned. It was too late to say she was sorry, that embarrassment and fatigue had caused her to overreact.

She had already lost a friend.

CHAPTER EIGHT

Back at the Adjutant General's office in Fort Leavenworth, Lt. Col. Amos Powell accepted the military pouch from his aide with grave foreboding. It had arrived from Fort Griffin by special courier only that morning. It could mean disaster.

He dismissed his aide and held the scarred leather in his hands, turning it over thoughtfully before extracting the papers inside. Inwardly, he was steeling himself for bad news. Maybe one of his undercover operatives had been killed, or discovered, or given up on the job.

So when he actually sat down and began to read the pompous ramblings of Second Lt. Kirkwood Fox, Amos Powell started to chuckle. The sound rumbled out of him like an avalanche, only a skittering suggestion at first, building to an earth-thundering roar.

To: Lt. Col. Amos Powell, Adj. Gen.
Fort Leavenworth Territorial Command
Kansas

In order not to bring disgrace on the army, I deem it

my duty to report the scandalous behavior of Operatives *A*, *B* and *C* while purportedly carrying out their assignments, vis a vis Fort Griffin and the Flats.

Although bona fide instructions suggested that Operative *A* seek employment as a dealer of faro, at no time was it indicated that she seek such employment at a place that also blatantly employs harlots. I feel I must warn you that, although acceptable gambling halls were available to her, she sought a den of iniquity specializing in ladies of the night.

When I attempted to bring this unseemly choice of establishments to Operative *A*'s attention, she refused to heed me, whereupon Operative *C*, traveling in the guise of a buffalo hider, womanizer and gambler, soundly punched me out before I could put the matter to rights.

Since I am currently under orders not to recognize Operative *C*, a situation I trust you will rectify, I had no recourse but to drop the matter until you empower me to act with at least a severe reprimand on behalf of the army.

In the meantime, Operative *B* has reverted to a savage state and appears to be imbibing large quantities of whiskey while working as a swamper in the aforementioned den of iniquity. The Indian's state of inebriation makes it impossible for him to give me coherent reports in spite of my repeated insistence and admonitions.

As for Operative *A*, her intemperate behavior has brought her the attention of one of the most notorious scoundrels in the Flats—who I can attest is a blackguard and a cheat at poker—and this, while in the service of the U.S. Army!

In view of the above, I would recommend that Operatives *A*, *B* and *C* be discreetly retired from active duty before bringing further disgrace on the army, and that the case be turned over to a Major Newcomb and myself at Fort Griffin.

April 15, 1874   Fox

By the time he was finished, Amos Powell had to wipe his eyes. He could imagine that little prig Fox being roundly decked by Landrum Davis. In fact, Amos thought, it was a shame he could not give Davis a special commendation for his actions.

Fox's report had Amos feeling almost exultant. The team was doing just as he had hoped they would do, fitting into the rough and tumble army post town.

As far as Amos was concerned, the fact that Celia was working in a place that also ran women was a big plus. The corruption at the Flats was tied up with the houses of prostitution. Powell would never have told Celia to seek out such a place, but he was pleased. He had thought Celia had the gumption and she was proving him right.

As for Glidinghawk . . . well, he had told Amos that although he drank rarely, he could always use the cover of a drunken Indian. People expected it, Glidinghawk had told the lieutenant colonel. Preston Fox was certainly taken in by it. Amos chuckled again, picturing the fresh-faced lieutenant trying to extract information from the stony-faced Indian.

Davis . . . Amos knew about his temperament, but he also had faith in his judgment. Amos had not been sure what cover Landrum would choose, but buffalo hider seemed perfect, giving him the leeway to spend time in the saloons.

Yes, Amos thought, things seemed to be shaping up. Briefly, he wondered just how much money Fox had lost to the blackguard he had mentioned—and hoped it was a considerable amount. Men like Fox deserved to lose.

And Celia . . . well, if she was having an affair with the cardsharper, so much the better. Davis and Glidinghawk would see that she came to no harm, and the army could scarcely expect her to act the part of a gambler without the experience to match.

Amos nodded to himself, musing on how his team—Powell's Army—had done so far. He picked up the calendar on his desk and made a note of the date Fox had sent the report.

Two weeks ago. It was now the first of May, 1874.

Amos had forty-five days before he would be called on the carpet about his undercover team. They might just make it in time—if Fox did not interfere.

He picked up his quill pen, considering a reply. He put it down on his desk again. Let Second Lieutenant Fox stew. The idiot had been warned not to make contact unless he had grave or important information to impart.

This, Amos concluded, was amusing, but not important.

Powell frowned. He wondered who this Major Newcomb at Fort Griffin was. Reading between the lines, Amos could tell that Fox was toadying up to the man.

Amos made a mental note to look up Newcomb's records and ask a few questions. Anyone Fox liked was automatically suspect in Powell's mind.

Fox was a poor judge of character.

CHAPTER NINE

Over the course of several weeks, Celia became adjusted to her job. Her feet stopped hurting and she found it was not difficult to sleep past noon every day and stay up all night. Everyone in town had taken to calling her Red. Sometimes, after work, she would join the others making the rounds of honky-tonks.

A dealer's greatest stumbling block to prosperity was his own addiction to games of chance, and Celia was not immune. She was making more money at the Brazos Club than she ever dreamed possible, and losing it just as quickly after work.

Over the madam's protest, Samuel had started paying her a twenty-dollar gold piece a night, matching the offer she had received from the Bee Hive.

After a night in which she lost forty dollars, Black Jack walked her home in the early morning hours. At first, she had been sure he found her highly desirable, but since that first night he had acted more like a courtly older brother than a suitor.

She had not been alone with him until now, or seen him as often as she would have liked. When they ran into each other at one of the gambling halls, he bought her a drink, but he had not pursued her. It was frustrating.

"The Flats are buzzing about the lucky streak you've been on since the big poker game," she told him.

"Don't I know it," he laughed. "I think the most popular wager in town is how much I've won."

"Maybe. . . ."

"Maybe what?" he asked.

He had parlayed that win into a fortune, which folks speculated might run as high as $50,000. Since it happened just after she arrived in town, Celia wanted to think she had brought him luck. Or she wanted him to think so. She had decided she wanted him.

"Maybe I turned your luck!" she said.

"Then it is about time I refreshed that lucky charm," he said. Tonight, he had backed off a game. He had asked Celia to leave with him.

"You know, Celia"—Black Jack was one of the few who still called her by her proper name—"you are falling into the trap of the born gambler. Hell, gal, I should know. I've been there all my life. You threw away your money tonight."

"I felt like playing," Celia protested. "Besides, I can afford to lose."

"Maybe . . . but you knew the table at the Golden Mount was crooked. Playing a crooked table is a fool's game."

"True," Celia agreed, her eyes sparkling, "but I think I can beat it. I know how that dealer plays his cards now. Next time, I'm sure I can win."

Black Jack sighed. Women beckoned from doorways, until they saw Celia. A few stragglers cat-called. The Flats late at night no longer seemed as threatening to Celia, especially striding along beside the tall gambler. He paused and struck a lucifer, lighting a quirlie. The flickering flame illuminated his face.

Celia genuinely liked him, and she had not forgotten the feeling of his lips pressing against hers. Many nights she had wished he would force his attentions on her, but he would only stop to talk and give her advice, without making any advances.

He stared down at her, lost in thought. "You remind me of myself—and that's not always good. I have money now, and for once I'm going to do something with it. And I have a few things to say about the way you've been carrying on lately."

Celia started to tell him that what she did was none of his business. On their infrequent encounters, he was critical of how completely she had swung into this gaming lifestyle. She did not want lectures from Black Jack.

At times, when Celia saw Gerald Glidinghawk at the Brazos Club, cleaning up after the careless men who missed the mark with spittoons—and then aimed kicks in the ragged Indian's direction—she felt bad about all the money she was making and wasting.

Black Jack tilted Celia's head up. He said gently, "When a man reaches thirty-five, he gets thoughtful. I wasn't intending to criticize. It's just tonight, I turned down a poker game with Major Newcomb, and it's about the hardest thing I've ever done. I feel like my lucky streak is over, unless I find a way to make it last. I've been putting out feelers about maybe becoming a business-man."

"You?"

"Well, it's happened to worse men. I can buy up a large part of this town . . . real estate. And instead of being a hawk on the wind with everything I own in my hip pocket," he gestured to the pocket where Celia knew he kept his gold, diamond-studded Jurgensen watch, "I can be somebody. . . ."

Celia wondered why he was telling her this, after treating her like a naive and errant younger sister when he talked to her at all. Did it mean he thought of her as something more? There was nothing worse than deciding to say *yes* to a man, Celia found, and not having him ask.

Now, the thought that he might have other things in mind when he looked at her made Celia's heart pound. She would be spitting mad if he did not at least kiss her good night.

A drunken yowl rent the air. Celia shivered.

"I guess we'd better be going," Black Jack said, putting his arm around her shoulders. "I hope that wasn't another damned fool getting himself killed."

They both craned their necks, but it was impossible to tell where the sound had come from. Besides, many strange yowls shattered the peace; it went with the territory. There wasn't a night that went by that at least one soldier didn't get himself cut or wounded in a brawl.

The clerk handed them their keys without a second glance. Their footfalls sounded on the stairs. The hotel was quiet tonight. Celia's room was up the corridor from Black Jack's. He walked her right up to her door. Then he hesitated.

"You have any whiskey in there?" Black Jack asked. "I could use a shot."

"I . . . well, I do keep a small bottle of medicinal

brandy," Celia faltered.

"Would you mind?"

His question was about more than a drink, Celia realized. She had been thinking of this moment for weeks. "No," she said softly.

He took the key and fitted it in the lock. Out of habit, he entered first, throwing back the door and checking behind the wardrobe before motioning for her to enter.

She laid her things—shawl, small handbag and derringer—on the bedside table. He lit the lantern. The room suddenly seemed very small.

Besides the narrow bed, there was only one straight-backed chair in the cubicle. He sat on it while Celia dug into the bottom of the veneered wardrobe for her medicinal flask.

"I . . . uh . . . I hope this is all right," she apologized. "I don't have drinking glasses."

"It wasn't really a drink I wanted," he said. "If you had turned me away I would be heading right back to that game, and I have a feeling this would be an unlucky night for me. That major is looking to skin me alive. . . ."

"Word is that you skinned him."

"It was an honest game," Jack mused. "Maybe Lady Luck didn't like him any better than I did."

The conversation did not relax Celia. She sat stiffly on the edge of the cot. To have a strange man in her room was about as close to perdition as she had come.

She did not want to tell him that she was a virgin. Possibly, he suspected as much. And he certainly would find out. But after tonight, Celia thought, she wouldn't be cursed with the problem any more.

"Something wrong?" he asked. "You're scowling at

95

me already. I can't figure you out."

"Don't try . . ." Celia began. But further words were muffled by his muscular body descending on hers.

Afterward, Celia stared at the ceiling, afraid to look in to his eyes. In the lantern light, the ceiling, which usually looked yellowed, looked decidedly pink. A glow suffused her. It was like nothing she had ever experienced before.

Finally, he spoke. "You surprised me, Celia. Virgins are about as rare as honest gamblers."

"Well . . . does it matter?"

"No," he chuckled. "Maybe I'm just curious. There's a lot about you I can't figure."

"Do you have to?"

"No. I just wouldn't let it get around that you aren't nearly what you seem. I saw you the first few nights, working at the club. You faked it some, but you weren't a professional dealer before, were you?"

Celia laughed uneasily. "A woman needs some mystery."

She suddenly wanted to tell him everything, but she knew she couldn't. She had to keep reminding herself of how important her job was. So far, she hadn't made much progress, except for fitting into life at the Flats.

"You like the gambling life, don't you?"

"Yes," Celia replied honestly. "I'm not sure I would want it forever, but I do like it. It's free and exciting."

"After a while, it . . . well, maybe I'm just getting old. This time next month, if a deal I'm working on goes through, maybe I'll own something and—"

Celia shushed him with a kiss, but not because she didn't like what she was hearing. It was the kind of thing every woman wanted to hear from her first man . . . but she did not want to hear it now. She was too vulnerable. If he asked her now, she would pledge herself forever.

Later, she wished she had let him talk. But then, their first night together, Celia thought they had all the time in the world. She thought passion like this could last forever.

She thought Lady Luck was smiling on them both.

CHAPTER TEN

Because of Celia's shift at the Brazos Club, and the erratic hours Black Jack kept, Celia still did not see him as often as she would have liked. When she was behind her faro bank, and he walked through the batwing doors of the club, she felt her heart swell with pride.

He was the best-looking man in the Flats, Celia thought. She liked the way he dressed, the way he smiled, the way he talked and acted like a gentleman—except in bed. She loved the feel of his warm skin against her own. She floated through her work, counting the hours until she would be free to be with him.

When he stopped by her table to tell her he was leaving town for a few days, she was heartbroken. He did not say where he was going, or when he would be back.

Celia had no ties on him. She realized, then, that she knew very little about him. Sometimes, he had mentioned the big poker games in New Orleans, but that was as close as he came to revealing anything of his past.

She was in a thoroughly bad mood when Samuel Wallace called her into the back room after work. Her fellow dealers watched her disappear and whispered about it. Samuel had been drinking more heavily than usual, and he slurred his words.

She thought she heard Lucky Jim say, "When he's this sotted, old Sam would jump a sow pig."

Interviews with Wallace were not pleasant at the best of times. He placed his arm on Celia's shoulders and squeezed. "Ouch," she said, twisting out of his grasp. "What did you want to see me about?"

For once, Celia wished Madam Agnes would come snooping around, but the madam was ensconced at the bar, drinking with Major Newcomb. What the major and the fat madam had in common, Celia could not figure, but they often had a drink together.

"Oh, nothin' special," Samuel said slyly, ignoring Celia's rebuff. He extracted the brandy and glasses from the desk drawer. He knew Celia liked the good quality brandy. He poured without asking.

"Then I shall be going," Celia announced, trying to be firm. "I am tired tonight."

Wallace chuckled. "I bet you are, Red." He thrust a glass in her hand. "Too many sessions with your fancy man."

"That," Celia said, haughtily, "is none of your business."

"Oh, I thought you and me was friends, especially after I got you that raise. Many men around here don't earn that much money in a month of Sundays. Thought you'd appreciate it."

Celia tossed back the brandy and slammed the empty glass down on Samuel's desk. "That was business, as I recall. I could have gotten the same from the saloon across the street. And my table is making more money than any two tables put together."

"If you aren't high and mighty," Samuel said, his eyes

reddening in anger. "You better watch your step. I just wanted to give you some friendly type advice. . . ."

"Such as?" Celia said, turning to leave.

"Don't you go putting too much store in that Black Jack. He sure was fired up about our Nellie before you came along. And you know as well as I do that a gambling man is here today and gone tomorrow."

"Is that a fact," Celia said coldly. Inside, she was seething. Of course she assumed Black Jack had known other women before she arrived, but she had never wanted to know the details. She would rather it were anyone but Nellie, who made her contempt for Celia plain.

Samuel lurched forward, spewing his whiskey breath into Celia's face. It could have knocked a fly dead from ten feet away. He pressed his body into hers, panting, "And I wanted you to know if you get lonely while your man is away, you can call on me."

Celia squirmed away from him. He anticipated her move and closed in. She stomped on his booted foot—hard. He jerked his leg back and muttered, "You're no better than any of these pigs."

Celia fled.

She hoped Samuel was too drunk to remember any details, because she did not want him to wonder why she had not taken the Bee Hive up on their offer.

She was afraid it was perfectly clear that she would rather work for anyone but Samuel Wallace. He was, she decided, the most repulsive specimen she had ever run across. For the first and last time, Celia had a speck of sympathy for his wife, Madam Agnes.

*   *   *

The days—and nights—stretched out forever. There were no more killings, but the night following payday twenty soldiers of the Sixth Cavalry reported that they had been drugged and robbed in the pigpens.

Black Jack had not returned. Celia heard a rumor from Lucky Jim, who heard it from a dealer at the Golden Mount, that he was holed up in a poker game. She was getting distinctly annoyed.

Major Newcomb strongly suggested that several shady ladies leave town. He and several other military men escorted them to Ben Ficklin's Mail and Stage Line. One prostitute begged money from the passers-by for her fare.

It was a good show of cleaning up the town, but Celia heard through the local grapevine that more soldiers were robbed after the women left. They had not looked like bad types to Celia, only worn and tired.

Celia went about her business, but her mind was on Black Jack. When she finally heard his special knock on her door at dawn one morning, she was torn between anger and desire. Desire won.

"I've missed you," he said, enfolding her in his strong arms. "Oh, Celia, you are a sight for sore eyes."

She was dressed in her nightgown. Her long red hair spilled down her back. Sleep marked her face. She entwined her limbs with his, but he pushed her away.

"Come on and dress," he said. "Let's get out of here. I've had enough of barroom smoke and small hotel rooms. I have a horse and buggy downstairs. Let's take a ride."

"You mean it?" Celia said. She had not been out of the Flats since she had arrived. Her world had become the saloons and hotel and eatery. The idea of getting away was very appealing.

She dressed quickly. Her feet flew down the stairs as she followed him. Outside, as promised, a small buggy was waiting. Black Jack helped her up and got in beside her.

"There's a spot not far from the river I like, a little north of town. Shall we?"

Celia smiled in answer. He took the reins and urged the horse forward, away from the clapboard, false-front buildings. In the hush of dawn, the cribs were silent. Celia knew that the saloons were open, but they did not tempt her or Black Jack.

When they passed the last shanty, to the north of town, Celia let out a whoop. "Fresh air," she said. "I forgot what it was like."

"Do you think it might be bad for us?" Black Jack asked, his mood matching hers. "I brought some whiskey and quirlies along, just to make us feel at home."

"What else did you bring?

"Me. Isn't that enough?"

Celia quieted. "I was beginning to wonder if you were coming back. Are you going to tell me where you were?"

He stopped the buggy. By now, they were past civilization, on a slight rise overlooking the Brazos. The river was a deep rust-red and flowing freely. Later in the summer, Celia had been told, it would dry up to a thin trickle. It was, even now, more stream than river.

Black Jack stared out at the water without answering. When he spoke, his voice was guarded. "Remember when you said a woman needs some mystery about her? Well, a man does too. I have some things I want to say to you, but they can wait . . . I hope."

As he always did when he wanted to stop argument or discussion, he covered her lips with his own.

103

"Maybe we should have stayed in my room," Celia said moments later, her words muffled against his coat.

"I came prepared," he said. He lifted a neatly folded army blanket out from behind the seat and alighted. He tied the horse to a mesquite tree and scooped Celia up in his arms as if she were lighter than air. He carried her ten paces, into a hollow protected by brush. There he unceremoniously dropped her, so that she found herself clinging to him for support. He laughed from deep in his throat, kissing the side of her head. "Oh Celia, I have missed you."

As they arranged the blanket, he pulled her off balance and she toppled with him to the ground. And they wrestled each other until their fight suddenly became an urgent need for one another.

Celia hated to head back to town. As they neared the Flats in the early afternoon, he stopped the buggy for a moment. Black Jack's face was as clouded as the sky.

"I thought this would be as good a place as any to settle," he said, "but maybe I was wrong."

"It's hard to believe, looking at it from here, that men are making a fortune there, isn't it?" Celia said. She was curious, but trying hard not to pry.

"Someone is," Black Jack said, strangely grim. "And he doesn't want any interlopers. One person owns most of that—whorehouses, saloons, town lots. And whoever it is doesn't want any competition."

"Who?" Celia asked.

"That I'd better keep to myself for now."

"Like you do everything else," Celia commented, her mood darkening like the day.

She had a difficult time at her table that night. Several soldiers accused her of stacking the deck. They were drunk, of course, and kept playing, but their complaints created a ruckus.

Black Jack did not stop by to walk her home.

Instead, Glidinghawk appeared like an apparition from a back alley. Celia had her tiny derringer cocked and aimed before she recognized him.

"Do you have any new information for us, or have you forgotten our mission?" he asked. He looked weary and haunted, as if his disguise had become a part of him. His proud, carved-idol face looked drawn.

Celia felt a stab of guilt, just as she did every time she saw him swamping at the Brazos Club. The men treated him like dirt, openly hating him because he was a red man. The women were almost worse; they ignored him the way they would a stray dog.

"I'm working on it," she whispered nervously. Even to her own ears, her reply sounded lame.

"Well, maybe you'd better work a little harder," Glidinghawk said. "Get off your high and mighty perch and start making friends with the whores. They ought to talk—and not all of them are stupid."

Celia colored. Glidinghawk was right; she had no reason to judge the women who sold themselves. It irked her to hear it from him, though.

She was going to make another excuse, but he was gone. On a day that had started out so beautifully, Celia found herself alone in her room with her guilt and doubt for company.

CHAPTER ELEVEN

Celia stopped by the Brazos Club the following afternoon. She headed directly over to the table where the saloon girls—including Nellie Vernon—waited for their first customers. Celia still had several hours before her shift.

Nellie did not like Celia. As queen of the prostitutes, she had a certain standing at the Brazos Club and throughout the town. Men made a fuss over her and paid top dollar for her favors. They talked about her beauty, her perfect oval face, buxom chest and high-stepping legs.

And Nellie was gorgeous. Celia had life to her, a certain piquant twist to her mouth that went well with her smattering of freckles. Her hair was gloriously red and memorable. But she lacked the glacial cool beauty of the blond with the icy blue eyes.

Celia knew this, and it did not bother her one bit. The trouble was, it bothered Nellie a lot, so much that she constantly whined to Madam Agnes about Celia.

"Men would rather lose their money to that floozy than buy my time," was the way Nellie put it.

Although that was not totally true, quite a few had fun

at Celia's table. She had diverted them from mooning over Nellie, whom most of them could not afford anyway. Besides, the soldiers were aware that their murdered brethren had been jinxed by time in the sack with Nellie.

So when Celia sat down at the whores' table, Nellie curled her perfect lips down and looked madder than a wet hen. Celia was not too happy either, but Glidinghawk had been right: she ought to at least try making friends with the working women.

"Are you going to be one of us now? Or don't you have it in you?" Nellie taunted.

Celia tried to be pleasant while she considered her ploy. She smiled and told the women, "Madam Agnes has mentioned several times that all of you dress so much better than I do. I was wondering if any of you could recommend a dressmaker."

Nellie continued to chew on her lower lip, but the others thawed. Colored Susan started to say something, when she was interrupted by Big Lil. "I use the same dressmaker Nellie does. The woman has been our little secret, but . . . well, she could use the money right now."

Nellie snorted. "Why don't you keep your mouth shut, Lil. Or pretty soon we'll be calling you Big Nose Lil."

Lil colored. Celia had heard that Nellie had a way of making life unpleasant for the women she did not like, possibly because she was in tight with Madam Agnes.

"Suds Row Annie could use the money right now," Lil defended herself. "And I, for one, would like to see her get more business."

Nellie caught a glimpse of Black Jack strolling through the door. He was headed for the bar. The way the tables were situated, he had not seen Celia.

108

"Excuse me," Nellie said, shooting daggers, "but I know a handsome gambling man who could be talked into buying me a drink."

Black Jack bellied up to the bar with his back turned. Celia wasn't about to make a ninny of herself by calling out, so she just fumed when he turned to Nellie, who was tapping him on the shoulder. The women were silent as they saw him smile and order another drink. Nellie had her charm fully turned on, and he was laughing easily.

Celia's pang of jealousy surprised her. He had hinted without making promises. Until now, she had tried not to take Samuel Wallace's words seriously. Sometimes Celia thought she could not get enough of the tall, easy-smiling man. Could Nellie feel the same way?

Black Jack's mysterious business and late-night games bothered Celia at times. It seemed to her that he was trying to hide something from her. But she had kept her mouth shut and reminded herself that she had a job to do.

Big Lil said, "Well, that don't mean nothing, honey. Any man who's asked is going to buy Nell a drink, unless he's flat broke. And everybody knows your man is in high cotton these days."

Your man. In spite of herself, Celia's heart thrilled to that. She felt the sympathy of the women enfolding her. Nellie was top dog, but she was not necessarily well liked. Celia saw Glidinghawk out of the corner of her eye. "About that dressmaker . . . ," she said.

The women started chattering, giving Celia advice on colors and yardgoods and styles. The mercantile carried a good grade of taffeta, they told her. One of them thought pink was right pretty on a redhead, but another said it had to be green. They all agreed that Nellie was more stylishly turned out than any of them.

Big Lil said, fuming a bit, "It's about time I let on about me and Nell's dressmaker. I've got a right to tell. She was a washwoman, same as so many out at the fort, married to Seth Downey."

A hush fell on the table. They all knew how brutally Seth had been murdered, as well as they knew the fate of frontier widows. Usually left without a dime, more than one *nymph du prairie* had once been a respectable married woman.

"She could get married again in two minutes," Colored Susan pointed out. Everyone knew that men at the fort would marry just about anyone who wore a skirt—if they got the chance.

The way the military operated, a certain number of men were given permission to marry—but just enough to fill the quota of washerwomen so necessary for keeping the soldiers' spit and polish. The washerwomen earned maybe half as much as their husbands. Between the two of them, a couple could manage a life, of sorts. That's why the married men's quarters were known as Suds Row.

Big Lil laughed, her huge bosoms heaving. "Two things there. First, Annie Downey is about as ugly as a sowbelly hog . . ."

"When did that ever stop one of them soldiers?" a homely girl named Gertrude asked.

". . . with teeth like a picket fence," Lil continued. "Second, she told me herself that after Seth she had had it with wifely duties, if you get my drift. He beat her up really bad and Annie don't want no more men in her life."

"How can a woman make it, then?" Colored Susan asked.

"Annie's ugly, but she sure is good at sewing. Not just buttons on uniforms, but dresses. The way everybody found out, Annie heard Major Newcomb wanted to get a dress made for Nellie, just like in this picture from Paris, France. . . ."

All the women looked dreamy at the mention of the fashion capital. They were also enthralled by a major making a special gift to one of them. Nellie might act like she was better than they were, but she sold her body the same as they did, even if a major was sweet on her.

"So Annie said she could do it and she did," Lil concluded. "It's that red satin dress of Nellie's, the one with the big bustle in back. Genuine silk."

Celia oohed and ahed along with the rest of them. This was interesting, indeed. Nellie and Major Newcomb. She had seen the proper military man. He often stopped in for a drink with Celia's nemesis, Lt. Fox, but she had not known about his liaison with Nellie. She wondered if Black Jack and the major had become rivals at more than the poker table.

"How did you find out?" Colored Susan asked.

Big Lil heaved again with mirth. "You can bet Nellie didn't share her find. Seth used to be a customer of mine. And though I know it isn't nice to speak poorly of the dead, he was a real lout. He promised me that his wife would make me a dress, joking like, if I'd give him a little extra."

"I'd like her to make me some dresses," Celia said.

Big Lil hesitated as Celia extracted paper and a pencil from her handbag and started to hand them over. Realizing her mistake—that Big Lil could neither read nor write—she said smoothly, "If you could tell me where Annie lives now, I will write it down."

111

"She's still in quarters at the fort, but they're goin' to make her leave unless she gets hitched."

Celia listened to the genuine interest the women took in Annie's plight. Lil was beaming as she recited Annie's tale of woe. She was the center of attention, since she knew more gossip. Celia realized that these women, unlike Nellie, did not dislike her.

Further, Celia was enjoying herself. Almost. From the corner of her eye, she saw Nellie rubbing up against Black Jack. When Celia finally left, the two of them seemed to be having a fine time.

Celia had not ventured to the fort before. There was a line of demarcation—the military post with its imposing fence, and behind it the officers' proper wives and the enlisted men's less proper ones.

The Suds Row wives were looked down upon. Many had been brought out west sight unseen, and they were often both uneducated and unattractive. But in the pecking order of an army post town, they also kept their distance from women tainted by the Flats.

Any woman associated with the Flats—with the rare exceptions of those who attended church at the fort and hid behind their draperies—were considered trash. A man who might play Celia's table and jolly her up at night, would not acknowledge her presence by day.

But she had an avenue of approach to a mission at a standstill, and she fully intended to follow it up. Lately, she knew she had been letting both Landrum and Glidinghawk down.

"Sir," she firmly told the guard, a man who lost

112

regularly at her table, "I am here to see Suds Row Annie."

He stared straight ahead, chin held high, trying not to look at her. "I must check with the major," he said.

"Please do."

Celia stood in the broiling sun. From inside the gates, she thought she caught sight of Preston Kirkwood Fox. Fox had stayed away from her since the night Landrum Davis had punched him out, but he drank at the club as often as Major Newcomb did. He had avoided Celia.

So she was extremely surprised when he strode over to her and said, "Come with me. The major wants to see you."

"But I came to see Suds Row Annie," Celia protested.

"This isn't like the Flats," Fox said stiffly. "If the major says he wants to see you, you obey."

She had little choice. As Celia walked at the lieutenant's side, she unconsciously imitated his marionette walk. He noticed.

As soon as they were out of earshot of the guard, Fox turned to her and hissed, "I will of course inform Lieutenant Colonel Amos Powell that you had the audacity to walk openly into the fort. . . ."

Though nobody could hear, Celia knew military posts. The place would be buzzing. Right now, she sensed the eyes observing them. She attempted a laugh, as if she were flirting. Fox was the last man in the world she would care to flirt with. She spoke softly, in lilting tones incongruous with her message. Her jaw ached from the effort.

"Look here, Fox, I will not have you making a spectacle of me. Pretend you are flirting with me, for

113

God's sake. You go ahead and diddle with your little reports. I am trying to follow a lead on the last murder. Smile, dammit."

Fox colored and grimaced, a pale imitation of a smile. At least he wasn't a complete imbecile. "When I get my message back from Fort Leavenworth, I think you will find yourself no longer working for the army . . . neither you nor that Confederate nor the drunken Indian."

"Until that time I have a job to do," Celia said. "And your job is not to interfere. I think this little talk has gone on long enough. . . ."

"Some job. Going to bed with a cardsharper. Just you wait," Fox muttered childishly, resuming his one-two-hup march to the major's office. His parting shot was, "I'm sure the major will put you in your place."

Celia was too stunned to reply. The fresh-faced officer was acting like a pompous fool. While she was certain the reports to Amos Powell were entertaining, they did cause her a moment's disquiet.

Fox saluted and left.

The major stood up to his full six-foot-two height. Celia had never been with him face to face before. She was startled by the clear, flinty blue of his eyes and the chiseled lines of his face. His skin was tanned and his lips thin but nicely formed under a clean upper lip.

"I don't gamble—on the faro tables, that is—so I have not had the formal pleasure. Major Newcomb, at your service."

Celia had chosen to forget how impressive an officer could be in uniform. Newcomb wore his well. He would look splendid in a dress parade and, in spite of herself, something about his complete, unquestionable authority

114

struck a responsive chord in Celia.

"But you know me?"

"Of you. Lovely Celia, the faro dealer. I'm sure my men have lost many of their paychecks to you."

Celia flushed. Of course they had. Even the army was not about to tell a man he couldn't drink or gamble off duty. "Is that what this interview is about?" she said lightly. "I had more frivolous things in mind. I wanted to see if Mrs. Downey—Annie—could make some dresses for me."

"Ah, and that brought an unfortunate situation to my attention," Major Newcomb said gravely. "She is going to have to leave the quarters of the fort. She refuses to . . . well, an unattached female can be quite a problem here. Perhaps you can suggest a room in town to her, where she would be available to her customers. She must leave here tomorrow."

"Are you suggesting I do your dirty work for you, Major Newcomb?" Celia asked sharply.

"I thought you might be sympathetic," he said. "Perhaps I was wrong. I assure you, I feel badly for the widow, but I do have a military post to run."

Celia questioned her judgment. From what Black Jack had said, and what she had been able to see from a discreet distance, she assumed that the major was strait-laced and cold. Now, he appeared charming and concerned.

"Of course I will do what I can," Celia told him, warming when she saw the light of appreciation in his eyes. "I had only intended to have some dresses made, but perhaps that would help her."

Her mind was clicking along. She might as well see what she could do. She was certainly making enough

115

money to help the woman with a substantial order. And the other women had seemed very interested in Annie's dressmaking skills. "Yes, I will see what I can do," she promised. "Is that all?"

The major's eyebrows came together, as if in heavy thought. He paused for a moment, and said, "You seem to be a charming lady. Perhaps it is not my place to warn you, but the man you are seeing, Black Jack, is under suspicion for murder."

Celia's heart kicked the inside of her ribcage. She had no reason to trust Major Newcomb and, in fact, had reason to doubt him. She knew, as did everybody else in Fort Griffin, that the major had lost a great deal of money to Black Jack.

But he looked so sincere, as if it pained him to divulge this information.

I would know if I was sleeping with a killer, Celia thought. Then other, less comforting thoughts tumbled through her mind. The unexplained trips. The late night disappearances. The fact that her lover remained a stranger with a past he had never divulged.

It took her a moment until she could speak. Slowly, she asked, "Could you tell me why you have reason to suspect him?"

"My dear Celia," Major Newcomb said, "I have already said too much, swayed, no doubt, by your charm. I hope you will keep what I have told you to yourself— and watch yourself around him. I would be extremely dismayed if any harm were to come to you."

He stood to terminate their discussion.

Celia was surprised by the warmth and strength of the hand he extended. It promised comfort and understanding, particularly when he added, "If you have any

116

problems at all, please feel you can rely on me."

Suddenly, Celia did not know who to trust. She needed time to think. She needed to talk to Davis and Glidinghawk—although both had been distant and disapproving of her lately.

Most of all, she needed to flee from the major, because right now she was sure he could read the confusion roiling through her.

Though Celia knew the major's story might be nothing more than the fabrication of a sore loser, his apparent sincerity was disquieting. And Black Jack had looked so treacherous, smiling down at Nellie Vernon as if they had been very close for a long, long time.

CHAPTER TWELVE

Celia's contacts with Davis and Glidinghawk were brief. Davis was out hunting buffalo for days at a time. His buckskins no longer looked stiff and new when he came into the Flats. He would stop by to place some bets at Celia's table. His countenance had always been fierce, but it used to soften when he looked at Celia. Used to.

She saw Gerald every day, only it was not the well-spoken, Dartmouth educated Indian she had come to respect on the trail. He was a surly animal, insulted and kicked around by the saloon scum. He appeared to be drunk most of the time.

"Why does Samuel keep him on?" Celia asked Big Lil, who had become a good source of gossip and information. They had worked together in getting Suds Row Annie started in a modest dressmaking business. She now had a room in town, and orders from all the calico queens from the Brazos Club. Only Nellie was displeased.

"You ever hear of a swamper who wasn't bottom o' the heap?" Big Lil asked. "An Indian will work cheap and give everybody else somebody to hate."

The bitter irony was not lost on Celia.

She had not felt comfortable with Glidinghawk since

the Indian-hating words had spouted from her mouth. Even though her parents had been killed in an Indian massacre, she thought she had put the hatred behind her. She knew enough to realize that the Indians were fighting for their lives. She wished she could explain to Glidinghawk that she had not intended to insult him.

But it was impossible to communicate with him. When she exchanged a few whispers with him, he was more stony than ever. His words were terse and without warmth. She had hoped he would soften when she did as he suggested and finally made friends with the harlots of the club, but he only nodded sullenly.

She had no idea what progress the others had made. She felt isolated and scared. Right after Major Newcomb planted the seeds of doubt in her mind about Black Jack, her lover had helped them grow. Black Jack was either out of town or tied up in a game. Celia wondered if any of the games concerned Nellie.

Yet she was not ready to denounce him to the others. She was torn between duty and the remnants of their passion. She longed for him and she was afraid of him. And worst of all, he wasn't around to take it out on.

So when he reappeared at the club one night after a five-day absence, her temper flaired. He strolled in casually, while Celia was dealing, and took his place behind the crowd at her faro bank.

As a general rule, he did not bet her table. Poker was his game. There, Black Jack claimed, a man needed real skill. Faro might be king to most players, but he seldom played it.

Celia sensed his presence before she saw him. She looked up from a new deck of cards and scanned the house. Over at the bar, she saw the back of Bernard

Newcomb's head. As usual, Fox was with him.

Black Jack caught the movement of her eyes. The expression that crossed his handsome face made Celia shudder. In the second before he shifted his focus and grinned at her over the heads of the other players, it had been positively murderous.

"Place your bets, men," Celia said. Her line of patter while she dealt was a pleasant chant, hour after hour. She was glad she knew it so well. She was rattled now.

Black Jack eased his tall body in, assessed the plays left by a sidelong glance at the casekeeper, and tossed some chips on the ten. His interest was in the dealer, not the bet.

"I've got to see you tonight," he said urgently.

Had Celia not been angry with him, she might have sensed that something was wrong. Black Jack was a gambler by profession. He had never interfered while Celia was dealing. He always waited until after her shift.

But Celia was angry. Angry because he left town without telling her. Angry because she was scared. Angry because he had been enamored of Nellie Vernon, and probably still was.

Celia called the turn and dealt. Only the heightened color of her face showed that she had heard him. She scooped the losers' chips from the board. Farley, the lookout, was on the alert, beefy muscles tensed for action.

"Please, see me and let me explain," Black Jack entreated, placing bets on the board without even looking at what they were.

"Ah, I see we have a winner here," Celia said, paying out on a small bet a soldier had made.

She could feel Black Jack's intensity.

121

Only a week ago, she would have melted inside. Now, she wanted to lash out at him. Her thoughts flew around like headless chickens. Without losing her rhythm with the cards, she knelt forward and whispered hoarsely, "I am having a drink with Major Newcomb after my shift. Now either play like a gentleman or get away from my bank."

"Damnation!" he exclaimed, turning on his heel, not waiting to see if his bets had won. He strode angrily away toward the end of the long bar where Nellie was holding court. His bets lost. Celia felt numb as she added his chips to the pile belonging to the house.

Farley gave her an approving leer. Samuel Wallace, who had been watching from diagonally across the room, also smiled. It was a nasty smile of triumph.

The rest of the night whirled by. By now, Celia could perform by rote, without thinking. The house did well. Her inner turmoil did not affect her dealing.

Perversely, she hoped Black Jack would be around when she got off work. She had no intention of having a drink with the major, but she knew Black Jack despised the man, although he didn't mind taking his money in a poker game. Now she was sorry about what she had told him.

Maybe she could take a small break between deals, let Black Jack know she was willing to talk to him. Maybe he had good reasons for his actions. Maybe they would make up in a way Celia had become addicted to. Maybe after that, everything would be as it had been before Nellie and Major Newcomb had filled her head with doubts.

Automatically, Celia's slender fingers danced through her job. Deal, collect chips, occasionally pay out. Her motions were so automatic that she almost missed the twenty-dollar chip placed squarely on the queen.

"Be lucky for me, Red," the man said. "Give me a winning queen."

Celia's beat faltered.

Landrum Davis with a play on the queen. He did not change it. *Code: danger, but not immediate. Be on the alert to meet later.*

Almost imperceptibly, she nodded to him. She pulled the cards out of the dealing box. No queen yet. Drawn by Davis' urgency, by the unspoken signals that passed among gambling men, other bettors covered the queen with their chips.

Celia's attention was riveted on the square. One man coppered his bet with a coin, betting it to lose. It was not Davis.

Instead, Landrum pulled a strange act. He waved a coin over his bet, as if considering coppering it, then withdrew it. Celia guessed that meant this was more serious than a joint meeting. It meant she should not panic, but be ready to run if Landrum should suddenly change his signal.

Even at a crowded table, betting fever rose and fell. When it rose, a tension sizzled through the air and the bets became larger and wilder. It was as if a collective feeling raced through the men, urging them toward one particular card. In this game, it was the queen.

Farley had come closer so that he could keep track. Over a hundred dollars' worth of chips were now riding on the queen. The silence was tangible.

On the next turn, Celia slapped a card over the soda. It was a five, revealing the queen in the dealing box. A wheezing, chuckling outtake of breath signaled the win. Farley frowned as Celia dug into her bank to pay out.

Her standing instructions to handle such an event were to stall, use sleight of hand, and make sure the card lost. She had tried, but her fingers did not work right.

Davis, and the others who had followed his lead, had won. Celia had attracted the attention of the house, meaning Samuel and Madam Agnes. Farley scowled when he collected the bank to take over for tallying. "Guess I'd better tell them you muffed it," he muttered. "You coulda done better."

"I tried," she said irritably.

After that, her dealing took a turn for the worse. She could not concentrate or make her hands obey. By the time she had dealt her final card of the night, her nerves were strung tighter than the rawhide on a bow. Both Farley and her casekeeper were unhappy. For the first time, their table had lost money for the house.

She threw the last bank on the table along with the last deck of cards. She knew Samuel would be wanting a word with her. She saw the major sitting over a drink and wished she could join him. Davis had faded away. Glidinghawk was not in his usual post. Black Jack had disappeared—and so had Nellie Vernon.

"You talk to Samuel," she told Farley abruptly. "I am not up to it tonight. I'm leaving."

Celia walked slowly through the almost deserted streets. The late spring air was oppressive, adding to her disquiet. Rain had threatened all day but had not burst through. When it did, it would be a deluge. The atmosphere was thick with menace.

She thought she saw Glidinghawk in a shadow, but it was a soldier propped up like a dead man against a building. She shivered and walked on.

The hotel loomed ahead of her. She had expected contact before reaching her room. Inside, the clerk handed her the wrong key. The key to Black Jack's room. *So he was out somewhere,* she thought. She was about to exchange it for her own, when she reconsidered. This might be a lucky break for her.

It would not hurt to take a look. They had used her small room for their lovemaking, never his. She wondered if he was hiding something there—anything to help her make up her mind about him. Deep inside, she wanted to forgive him.

Her footfalls seemed eerily loud pounding down the hallway, though she walked with whisper-soft steps. She wanted to be quick. She saw another hotel patron and brazened past him, hoping that she did not look suspicious.

The key scratched in the lock and turned. The door creaked open. She immediately saw a shadow by the window—or thought she did. She flattened herself in a corner and waited until her breath came back, convincing herself that she had imagined it.

She lit the lantern, turning it up only enough for a feeble light. Her whole body quaked. She fumbled inside Black Jack's wardrobe. Aside from another fine suit and a spare flask, it was strangely barren. Celia took a deep drink and felt it burn courage right through her. Old Overholt.

Slightly calmed, she systematically rifled his pockets and found a torn piece of paper. She put it in her pocket to read later.

His valise was stored under the bed. She pulled it out and opened it. Inside, there was a locked case that she could not open. It looked like the valise of any man who did not have roots: spare handkerchiefs, a pair of cuff links and changes of underwear. Celia did not want to disturb the order. Black Jack was a neat man.

Under a small stack of spare collars, she saw a glint of steel and recoiled as if it had been a snake. It was a small but sharp knife. She recalled the description the cafe owner had given her . . . how long ago?

She heard the old woman's voice as if it were yesterday. "Poor Seth Downey, when they found him, his third leg—ha hah, that's a good one—was almost hacked off. Run through with a blade, he was, and a sorry sight. . . ."

Celia shivered uncontrollably, in spite of the jolt of whiskey she had just consumed. A lot of men carried knives. It did not mean that the major had been right. It did not mean that Black Jack was the killer.

Still, it took enormous effort for Celia to carefully lay everything back in the valise in neat stacks—collars, underwear, handkerchiefs, locked case. She shoved it back under the bed. Pills of dust skittered from her hands.

Her legs were so weak they almost buckled as she stood up. Blood rushed from her head. She fought to remain clear-headed against the fog that was overwhelming her. She felt sick.

Celia finally managed to make it to the door. She locked it and hurried to the stairwell, where she leaned against a wall until her strength returned.

She walked through the lobby to the front desk. "You gave me the wrong key," she said. "I wish you would be more careful."

The desk clerk hrumphed and exchanged keys.

"You people coming in day and night, doing God knows what—a man can make a mistake," he squeaked.

This time, the stairs were almost too much for Celia. Her legs seemed heavy and leaden. She tried to remember something, some message she had had on her mind earlier, but it eluded her.

Visions of Black Jack flashed through her mind. His gentle touch as he stroked her hair, the sight of his bare, muscular chest as he sat up in bed, the way his lips curled up in a smile just for her.

She remembered the night he had promised to stay with her, until his restless pacing drove her wild and she had almost shrieked as she told him to go. She recalled how haunted his eyes had been those nights when he started to speak and then fell silent.

There was so much about him she thought was explained by the wandering, secretive life of gambler—so much that she had thought she could accept as part of him.

But a cold-blooded killer she could not accept. She could not accept his apparent liaison with Nellie Vernon. And she could not accept that she had been taken in by his deceit.

When she let herself in her own room, stumbling blankly through the door, a hand closed over her mouth, stifling the scream in her throat.

Her struggles lasted only moments before blackness overtook. For the first time in her life, Celia Louise Burnett fainted dead away.

CHAPTER THIRTEEN

Celia was already fighting when consciousness returned. Her fingernails raked Glidinghawk's face and he spun back before grabbing her hands. She opened her mouth to scream. He pulled her so close that the sound was muffled against his shoulder. The scream changed to dry, harsh sobs as she recognized him. Her fists pounded against him, but it was the helpless, frustrated pounding of a child.

He cradled her head and whispered soothing sounds in her ear, sounds of comfort in a language she did not understand. "He has a knife," she cried, "I saw his knife."

"Quiet," Glidinghawk cautioned. "Calm down. Later. You are safe for the moment. Calm down. You can tell me later."

Celia clung to him like a drowning woman. The color came back to her face and the world righted itself slowly. She felt that she had made a mess of things from the beginning.

"I'm sorry . . . about everything," Celia said. She felt hollow inside. She had wanted to apologize to Glidinghawk for a long time, and there was so much else that she was sorry about. He was not listening.

"I want you to get dressed and come with me. I don't want you to stay here tonight. Come with me to meet Landrum. We'll be riding, but don't wear anything that will attract attention if someone sees you on the street."

He turned his back as Celia slipped on a plain broadcloth dress. She hated riding in a dress, but a woman in pants was unheard of. She had not been able to speak plainly with Gerald and Landrum since their last night on the trail. She had a lot to tell them—a lot that she dreaded telling them. She would let them know her lover was the killer. Perhaps they suspected. She was, after all, in danger. Was Black Jack planning to kill her?

"Can I turn around now?" Gerald asked, impatient and disgusted, though whether with her or himself, Celia could not tell.

"I'm ready. How should I leave the hotel?"

"You come out the back way with me. Take your key. My horse is hidden in a back alley. Follow behind but not too close, in case someone spots us. Do you understand?"

Celia knew that outside her window was a roof and a steep drop to the ground. She was terrified of heights. "Can't I stroll out the front door?" Celia asked. "I could meet you."

"No," Glidinghawk said. "There is a man who has been following you. He was in the lobby before I came up here."

"Black Jack?"

"No, not your lover," Gerald said harshly. "Come on. This is the best way."

He slipped through the open window and Celia followed. Once on the roof, she would not allow herself to look down. She crawled after the lithe Indian to the edge of the shingles. The drop was about seven feet.

"Now, you swing over the edge and jump. Keep your knees bent. It isn't far. If you want, I can hold you from here before you drop. Or I can go first and be waiting."

Either way, Celia didn't like it. Seven feet seemed a world away.

"Dammit, make up your mind."

"You first," Celia said.

He swung himself around and landed lightly as a cat. Inch by inch, Celia moved forward until her head was at a level with the line of the roof. He had made it look so easy. She looked down. Her head swam again.

She ducked back as she heard another man's heavy booted walk in the alley. "Goddamned Indian," a man cursed. There was a thud and a scuffle.

Celia was afraid to move. She was afraid she was stuck, unable to return to her room, unable to go forward. If it was Glidinghawk who had fallen, she was in deep trouble.

Then, she heard a sound like the hoot of an owl. It had to be him. Again, the call sounded. She forced herself to swing around and cling to the shingles. Suddenly, she was sliding, flailing and falling into a great void. Glidinghawk's arms caught her before she could cry out.

He grabbed her roughly and pulled her after him. She stumbled over the prone body of a townsman, the one who had tangled with Glidinghawk. Lying there, the man looked dead.

Glidinghawk silently motioned Celia forward. His small mustang was tethered a hundred feet away. He crept up to it and untied the reins, leaping on the animal's back. Less gracefully, Celia mounted behind him. Her arms clung to Glidinghawk for support.

On the outskirts of the Flats, Glidinghawk eased the

horse into a lope, and then a gallop. With every mile further away from the town, Celia could feel Glidinghawk's tensed muscles relax. By the time they reached the small camp where Davis waited, her grip loosened to a fraction less than a death hold.

There was no fire. Landrum had chosen a slope partially protected by mesquite trees. His horse, Lone Star, was tied to one. The mare that Celia had ridden down the trail whinnied at her approach. She wished she could expect as warm a reception from Davis.

Reluctantly, she let Landrum help her down.

There was a quarter-moon out, when the heavy storm clouds did not obscure it. Already, several raindrops the size of bullets had exploded across Celia's face. She joined the men in a small circle.

"I guess I don't have to call you Red out here," Landrum said. "Looks like a night made in hell, but this could not wait. They might be on to you and you are going to have to decide how to handle it."

"You mean Black Jack?"

"No. Unless you know something I don't." Landrum's piercing stare wilted Celia's resolve. She was going to come clean with everything she knew—or thought she knew—but maybe she could hear what the others said first.

"Who?" she breathed like a prayer.

Landrum swore softly. "Have you been paying any attention to our mission? Wallace. Wallace and that same low-down drifter we tangled with before we hit Fort Griffin. They are tied up somehow. Remember the man saw you back there? He's been playing at your table, following you around, cozying up to Wallace."

"I need to sit down," Celia announced, sinking to the moist earth. The others squatted on their haunches and waited. She fanned her face with her hands.

"This isn't the time for a weak-kneed female act," Landrum snorted.

Celia snapped her head up. "I had the house down my back all night, I broke into a man's room, I had Gerald barge in on me like a killer and I had to leap off a roof and ride all the way out here. And now you tell me my cover is blown. If that makes me a weak-kneed female . . . well, I'd like you to try a night like that!"

"I didn't mean to be so harsh," Landrum said. "Let's not let our tempers get in the way. The man who's been following you is named Simmons, or so he says. I don't know where he fits in. I do know that anybody in tight with Madam Agnes or that slimy husband of hers means trouble—and that includes Major Newcomb."

"And Black Jack?"

"What is it you have to tell us about him that we don't already know? I'm sick of hearing his name."

Celia said quietly. "The major told me that the army thinks he's the killer. I found a knife in his room tonight."

Glidinghawk shook his head. "That does not make sense. What kind of knife? A lot of men carry knives."

Celia knew small firearms, but all she knew about knives was that the butter knife was shorter and flatter. She said, "It ws about this long, and had a leather handle on it, and it looked sharp."

Landrum and Gerald exchanged looks. Celia could tell that they had become closer while she was risking life and limb in the Flats. Gerald, though he worked at the same

133

place she did, slipped in and out unnoticed—no doubt carrying tales of her every action. It was maddening and humiliating for them to come across with that masculine superiority now.

"Celia, your lover is not a killer," Landrum said. "Not even one of our suspects. The dead men were hacked up, but the job was done with a long, slashing instrument— probably a sabre."

"Thank God," Celia said almost tonelessly.

"It would be easier if he were," Landrum continued, trying for patience. "What we have so far is pretty much what we started with—except that Simmons might tell Samuel Wallace he saw you with us in strange circumstances."

Celia listened as well as she could. Her spirit was restored. Inside, she was singing. Everything would be all right. It had to be all right. She had been wrong about Black Jack, and that meant the major had been wrong about Black Jack, too. She would make it up to him. A shiver of anticipation ran through her.

"Someone at the fort is in on the killings, probably someone trained with a sabre. They seem random, but there's a logic behind them, I suspect, and it has to do with Madam Agnes' operations. She owns about half of the property in the Flats, she and Samuel, and runs every kind of pigpen known to man."

Celia was puzzled. She knew about the saloon girls, but could not remember what Big Lil told her had kept the Brazos Club girls in line. It was in the back of her mind like an itch she could not reach to scratch.

"But we have nothing solid yet," Davis sighed. "Somehow, the connection between the fort and the pigpens will come out in time—but we have to get rid of Simmons."

"I'd like to get the bastard myself," Glidinghawk said. "He came close to killing me. But it's not in our orders. There is only one way. . . ."

"Yes," Landrum said, nodding his head sagely. "If he were, say, to molest Celia, she would be within her rights to shoot him."

Celia's jaw dropped open.

She was too stunned to speak. They were suggesting—suggesting, she reminded herself, not ordering—that she kill a man in cold blood.

"There has to be another way," she protested.

Davis and Glidinghawk again traded silent communication. They both looked long and hard at her, as if assessing the relative merits of a defective weapon. She didn't like it one bit.

"Yes," Landrum said slowly, drawing out his words with that Southern accent of his. "You could drop out of the mission and let us handle it from here."

"Why can't things just go on the way they are? I'll keep dealing at the club and digging harder for information. That man, that Simmons, he hasn't said anything yet."

Her green eyes widened and she tried her damnedest to look appealing. They were placing her squarely in the middle. She did not want to kill. She did not want to give up. And, with them, there was no in-between.

Gerald spoke. "We all know that we are not empowered to kill. Officially. But there are times when there is damned little choice. Celia, you wanted to work for the army. You're part of the team, whether we like it

135

or not. And right now, I know Landrum does not like it any better than I do."

As they had been earlier, when he had calmed her hysteria, Glidinghawk's words were soothing, but completely at odds with the message they conveyed. Celia found herself listening and nodding.

It was odd that he was spokesman, while Landrum was mute. It was as if there had been a subtle change of power while Celia had been wrapped up in her life as a gambler. The two of them were now the leaders, and Celia was the pawn they were using.

Everything made sense, that was the God-awful part. She was the one in danger, and she was the one who could publicly gun down the man who knew too much. She had feared that Black Jack was a cold-blooded killer, and he was not. If she kept nodding and agreeing, she would be.

"Do you think you can do it?" Landrum asked.

"I . . . what—what did you say?"

"If it comes down to it, can you shoot Simmons?"

The fat clouds rumbled in the distance, blanketing the moon. It was pitch dark. A cool wind whipped Celia's face. She hoped the others could not see the tears forming in her eyes. She had to get hold of herself. She was made of sterner stuff.

She gathered her courage about her like a mantle. "You have both seen me in action. If someone threatens to kill me, I will shoot. But the decision is mine. I refuse to chase that man down and kill him without provocation."

Landrum groaned. "If you saw a snake, would you wait to see if it was rattler before you pulled the trigger? A snake is a snake. . . ."

"And he is after you," Glidinghawk said.

"This is not solving a damned thing," Landrum said. "I have half a mind to shoot the bastard myself."

"And get strung up for all the murders?" Glidinghawk said. "If it comes down to it, I can kill him more quietly."

"That citizen's group would love to scalp an Indian," Landrum said.

"More trouble in Paradise?" Celia asked sarcastically. "Anything you think you ought to bother my pretty little head about?"

"Nothing you wouldn't know if you'd been paying attention to anything but your fancy man," Davis said. "A fat banker by the name of Kiley wants the place respectable. He claims that if Major Newcomb can't clean up the town, a committee of vigilantes would be glad to do the job."

There was not much for Celia to say. She had sensed the Flats were like a powder keg about to go off—even Madam Agnes' girls were antsy—but she had not known the details.

"The Flats have no law but what a man takes into his own hands—or that imposed by a stiff-necked major who has the pressure on him. If either of us kills the man and is unlucky enough to get caught, we'll be the scapegoat for all the killing there. We won't stand a chance. A woman might."

"Wonderful," Celia spat out.

"Are you worried about your eternal soul?" Gerald chided. "Maybe you should have thought of that before. . . ."

". . . before I succumbed to a man's charms—other than your own, that is." Celia finished bitterly. She was beginning to believe that Glidinghawk had a streak of puritanism in him. It was the same as the one that she tried so hard to stifle in herself.

Landrum stood up and started walking back and forth, tossing words into the wind. "We are all acting like a bunch of amateurs. This is no place for the emotions of children."

"Hah!" Celia cried, jumping to her feet and chasing after Landrum. She pounded his shoulder and made him turn around and stop. "You meant *women* and children, didn't you? Let me tell you something, both of you. And don't you dare laugh, because it isn't funny. The two of you have been treating me like some dim-witted female. All of a sudden you want me to kill a man because I might be in danger. It doesn't make sense. If I were a man, what would you have me do?"

"Kill the bastard," Glidinghawk barked. Celia glared at him. The light might be bad, but she was sure he saw the sparks in her eyes.

Finally, Landrum said, "It isn't easy to treat you like a man."

"And if it comes down to it, it will not be easy for me to kill like a man," Celia said grimly.

CHAPTER FOURTEEN

Celia had no intention of killing Simmons. In her head, she was plotting every way around it. But that was before the powder keg called the Flats exploded in violence, and she was caught in a maelstrom of evil that swept her along with it.

She had managed to get back to town all right, returning to her room by the back window. The townsman whom Glidinghawk had knocked out wasn't in the alley anymore.

"I bet that's the last time he uses that alley for an outhouse," Glidinghawk whispered.

Celia giggled. She and Glidinghawk had not exactly made friends again—she doubted anything could erase the Indian-hating taunt she had flung at him—but they were back to being allies. She had been content to let her eyelids droop as she clung to him on the ride back.

"Take care of yourself," he said solemnly before they parted outside her window.

"You too," she replied.

Then she sank into a deep sleep that erased everything else. It was late afternoon by the time she awoke. Immediately, she had an uneasy feeling that something was wrong, but she tried to brush it aside.

Only nerves, she assured herself as she dressed for work. Nerves, and the weather—and that man who might blow her cover at any minute. The rain had started, and it was a deluge. It pounded on the ramshackle buildings and seeped into every crack. Outside, the streets were muddy streams.

She thought she should eat before work. The eatery two blocks down from the Brazos Club was consistently bad, but her stomach had adjusted to overfried buffalo steaks. She armed herself with an umbrella, planning to head there.

She was already in the lobby when a new onslaught of rain lashed down. Peering at the glistening wet boardwalk that, if the rain kept up, would soon be underwater, she wished idly that she did not have to go to work tonight. But she knew that the club would be busier than ever.

She backed into the shelter of the lobby. It was crowded for a change. Men and women were waiting out the latest gully-swamper in its shelter. She looked at the men around her. One face looked familiar. Scruffy, but not badly dressed, he was a man Celia had seen many times before and had thought nothing of. She had had no reason to fear him. Now, she knew he was Simmons.

Celia noted his checked, worsted coat, his close-set eyes and dark mustache. He was certainly not distinguished, except for a slightly crafty look across his plain face. Celia did not see a holster, but there was a bulge in the waistband of his pants. He was probably armed.

She was concentrating on him, and took little notice of the fat man in the vested suit, standing with another group of businessmen. They were more conservatively dressed than the gamblers and cowboys who, along with the soldiers, frequented the saloons. She hadn't seen such a sea of boiled shirts and starched collars since she had left St. Louis.

Simmons appeared not to notice her stare. Still, Celia figured she could find something better to do with her time than wait in the lobby for the downpour to cease. She forgot her hunger pangs. Maybe Black Jack would still be upstairs.

Perhaps it was the increased danger she was in, or the wild relief of finding that Black Jack was not a suspect, but Celia wanted him more than ever. She was willing to say she was sorry—something she had been doing a lot lately.

But this time, Celia wanted to do more than just tell Black Jack that she was sorry. She wanted to show him. She wanted to devour him.

She checked with the squeaky desk clerk and found that his key was not downstairs. She asked the correct time, and the pudgy man in the swell suit pulled out his fob with chilly politeness. If she skipped dinner, she had two hours before her shift.

Ample time for making up. Ample time for making love. She hoped he would be eager. She only wished, as she trudged back upstairs, that she could shake off the uneasiness that trailed her more surely than the grifter downstairs.

Her step lightened at the corridor. They had not yet whiled away a rainy afternoon together. Scenes of reconciliation flashed in her head. She knocked softly on his door.

"Black Jack, it's Celia," she called out softly.

She put her ear against the door but heard nothing except the fury of the rain. She called again. "About last

141

night. I am sorry. Please let me in."

Maybe he was sleeping. She tapped her foot impatiently against the floorboards. She knocked again. She wondered how long he had spent buying Nellie Vernon drinks after she had left the club. She rapped harder.

A whiskey-voiced woman from the next room rasped, "Keep it down, will you?"

Celia was sure Black Jack was in his room. She rapped three times loudly, two soft beats, three loud—the same signal he had used when coming to her room late at night . . . or early in the morning.

The frowzy harlot stuck her head into the corridor as Celia's fingers jerked at the doorknob. The door swung open. The first thing Celia saw was the sheet of rain blowing through the open window, making the curtains dance like frenzied ghosts.

In the blink of an eye, she saw Black Jack's hacked up body. He lay sprawled on his back, his throat slashed from ear to ear. Celia was transfixed by the darkening rivulets of blood that made crazy-quilt patterns down his naked, mutilated torso. His slate gray eyes stared straight ahead, locked in eternal terror.

Celia screamed.

Pounding footfalls sounded on the stairs. Fights and screams were the everyday sounds of the Flats, but this inhuman shrieking could make the hackles rise on a hardcase.

The harlot ducked inside her room and locked her door. When the men from downstairs converged on the scene, Celia was standing in the middle of her dead lover's room, screaming her lungs out.

The hotel clerk found a sheet and pulled it over Black Jack's mutilated body and terror-frozen face. Celia was in shock. The sounds babbling around her made little sense until much later.

"Better call the undertaker."

"The woman have any friends who can help? She's in rough shape. Who can get her out of here?"

"I'll send my boy over to the Brazos Club. Christ!"

"It's the stiff we got to worry about it."

"Send for the major over at the fort."

"I told you we need a tough town marshal."

"Last one got himself killed two months ago. You wanna apply for the job?"

"You know this man?"

"Did. Good gambler. Must have a fortune stashed."

"We ought to string up the fellow who did this. Whores, gamblers, killers . . . this is going to kill us in Washington."

"Did you see his. . . ."

"The lady. . . ."

"Some lady. Works in the club."

"Dealer, not whore."

"Same difference."

"Later. God Almighty, this one's worse than the last one. Did you see his. . . ?"

Celia's shrieks had subsided to harsh sobs. Somehow, Big Lil was by her side. "Come on, honey," the fleshy whore said, leading Celia away, "you've seen enough."

Meekly, Celia let herself be guided. Big Lil walked her down the hallway and opened Celia's door for her. She took her inside and gently pushed Celia's rigid body down to a sitting position on the narrow bed. Celia did not resist. She had no fight in her.

"You got any whiskey around?" Lil asked.

"In the wardrobe," Celia answered woodenly. When

Big Lil held the flask up to her lips, she drank. She remembered drinking on this bed with Black Jack. She drank again until the flask was empty. Big Lil sent out for more.

They heard the commotion in the hallway.

"Are they taking him away yet?" Celia asked.

Big Lil shook her head. Her black sausage curls swatted against her plump cheeks. "They're waiting for Newcomb." She made a sound like a fart deep in her throat. 'Like with the other killings, they don't got no law, so they turn it over to him. He makes reports and ain't nobody gets caught."

Celia started to rise, but Big Lil pushed her back. "Where do you think you're going? You stay right here in bed. Have another drink. You ain't never had anybody get killed on you before, have you? It's always hard, the first time . . . have another drink."

The whiskey was seductive. It warmed and numbed Celia down to her toes. It would be nice to lie here, she realized, and get so drunk that she could forget. But instead of melting and dissolving inside, she felt a cold white fury building. "I want to see what is happening," she said.

"Honey, you'd best try to forget."

"I'll never forget," Celia resolved, standing tall. "I am going to walk into that room and stay with his body until the undertaker gets there. He was my lover and I am not ashamed. I want to be with him."

"Awful lot of ghouls hanging around," Big Lil said. "And citizens that don't hold no store with women like me—or you. Are you sure you want to face them?"

Celia wiped at her tear-streaked eyes. "Yes. I'll understand if you want to return to work." She smoothed her hair back and adjusted the skirt of her dress.

Big Lil hesitated. Madam Agnes would be furious. Even murder did not come before work. Lil's heart was as big as her derriere, but Celia saved her from making the decision. "Just walk me down to his room," she said. "Then . . . this is something I have to do myself."

They both held their heads high. Big Lil had the stately walk of a fat woman. She swayed from side to side with every step. Celia looked frail alongside her. The gawkers parted to let them through.

That same stuffy man in the vested suit stood in front of the body. He had appointed himself as lead ghoul, Celia thought. "We don't need your kind here," he said.

Celia ignored him. She gave Big Lil a hug and whispered, "Thank you."

She heard Big Lil descending the stairs heavily. She placed a chair beside the body and sat down primly. Her eyes were dry. She defied any man to speak to her. She hated the way they stared, hated the gleam in their eyes because someone had been murdered and they were still alive.

Simmons was part of the crowd, but he backed away when he felt Celia singling him out with her hard eyes. The hotel clerk fluttered around, deferring to the plump man. When he squeaked, "I don't know how to get them out of here, Mr. Kiley," Celia made the connection with the banker Landrum had told her about last night.

"Don't ask them to leave, order them," Kiley said.

But the crowd did not disperse until Major Newcomb marched up the stairs. Then, the gawkers made themselves scarce, like cockroaches fleeing from a light.

The major was impeccably dressed. His posture was

straight and tall. He acknowledged Celia with a curt nod. "If you will be so kind as to leave, I want to examine the evidence," he said.

"I'll stay," she said firmly.

A muscle in his jaw spasmed. "As you like," he said, whipping the sheet from the corpse.

Celia could not bear to look at the hacked up, bloody body again. Instead, she gazed up at Major Newcomb. Beyond his iron-clad control, she saw the swift intake of his breath. She saw his lips go momentarily slack, and his eyes glaze over.

It was a look she had seen before, that she recalled from somewhere. She had seen it on Black Jack's face in the throes of orgasm.

Celia felt like screaming again. The major's hands trembled, poised above the body. He covered it again and tore his eyes away.

"Mr. Kiley, we must gather up his personal effects. You can be my witness on them. There are rumors he had a considerable amount of money . . . but we all know gamblers."

Major Newcomb seemed to be shaking himself out of a deep fog. "I would estimate he was killed late last night." He paused significantly, and asked the room clerk, "Can you tell me anything about his movements?"

"He was drinking with Nellie Vernon at the Brazos Club, last time I saw him," Celia volunteered. But surely the major knew that. He had been there.

"He returned to his room early—for Black Jack, that is," the clerk said. "I keep a good lookout for strangers, don't let much get by me. But there is something you ought to know, Major Newcomb."

Celia ignored the little man and tried to get a grip on

her feelings. She could not believe that she had been so stupid as to suspect Black Jack. His small knife could never have done so much damage. It had to have been a larger, sturdier weapon.

She fought to remain analytical, thinking only about the weapon and the timing and who might have broken in on him. She would find out who did it.

"So she came in and asked for Black Jack's key, and I thought, why not, because ever'body knows they got a thing going. . . ."

Kiley practically crowed, "I've told everybody that women like that will ruin this town. Now they will listen to me."

The words began to register.

Kiley, the hotel clerk, Major Newcomb and his aide surrounded Celia, staring down at her. Her mouth opened, but no words came out.

"Arrest her," Kiley demanded, rubbing his rotund middle with something akin to glee.

Strangely, it was Major Newcomb who defended her. She sighed with relief when he said, "I find it highly unlikely that a woman could have committed this murder."

Celia's rush of gratitude was quickly quelled when he added, "But, Miss Burnett, I will want to make further inquiries when you are up to it. In the meantime, do not leave town. If I find you have acted as an accessory, I will make sure you spend time behind bars."

CHAPTER FIFTEEN

Boot Hill or O'Neil's Ranch, whatever it was called, every town had a burying spot for the gunslingers, the itinerant gamblers, the whores and the riffraff. Fort Griffin was no different.

The cemetery was about a mile out of town, on a barren knoll overlooking the Clear Fork of the Brazos. It was not far from the spot where Celia and Black Jack had made love in the overcast light of dawn.

Black Jack was buried there in the rain-soaked ground on the following afternoon. A few poker cronies, members of the gambling circuit, lowered his coffin. Some women were present, with tears running down their painted cheeks. Celia was the only one among them without tears, having shed hers in private.

Her grief had changed to a steely resolve. She wanted his killer. She wanted revenge. When the prayers were said over Black Jack's body, Celia's inner words were far different from the bromides offered by the preacher-for-hire. She vowed to get the man who had murdered him.

"Thought you would be off work tonight," Samuel

said. "I was going to have Farley cover your table."

"I'd just as soon work, if that's all right," Celia said. She meant it. A night alone in her room would be intolerable.

"You know you can twist me around your little finger," Samuel said.

He had chosen to forget the argument they had the night he grabbed Celia in the back room. But every time the man talked to her, he ended up with spittle in his mustache. Celia found him disgusting—particularly when he pawed her with those damp, oily hands of his.

"Then I'll go set up," Celia said, quickly removing herself from his reach. Farley and Sneaky Pete were at her bank in deep conversation. They broke off as she approached.

"Back again?" Farley sneered, surly.

"Didn't your protector leave you lots of money?" Sneaky Pete taunted. "You still a working woman?"

Until now, the burly lookout and the sly casekeeper had managed to keep their resentment hidden. Celia was too popular at the Brazos Club. Secretly, they believed that her arrival had kept them from having a faro bank of their own.

"She's just here for show," Farley said. "Everybody knows she stole her fancy man's money before she killed him. She was afraid that maybe he'd leave it to Nell."

Celia spun around and leveled an angry gaze on Farley—her wide eyes narrowed to tiny slits of flashing emerald. "I'll thank you to keep your nasty little comments to yourself," Celia said.

"Yes, ma'am," Sneaky Pete said. "I sure wouldn't want to get on the wrong side of you."

Celia stepped behind her table and arranged the dealing box and cards the way she liked them. She knew that Pete and Farley were only repeating the gossip around town. The rumor that she had killed Black Jack had been fueled by the hotel clerk's lies.

The fact that no one could find the fortune that Black Jack was supposed to have somewhere didn't help her standing. Though the major required evidence to make a case against her, the rumormongers didn't. And, while technically a free woman, since the murder Celia had noticed a uniformed shadow dogging her every step.

Celia scanned the huge saloon and gambling hall. The callow youth who had been on her heels at the cemetery had been replaced by Second Lieutenant Preston Kirkwood Fox. Celia almost laughed hysterically.

More than once in the last twenty-four hours, she had felt her secret army papers burning a hole through the heel of her shoe. She hoped that she would not have to use them. One of the things that most concerned her about being under surveillance was that she would have no chance to consult with either Landrum or Gliding-hawk.

The string band tuned up their instruments. As usual, Celia winced. They were extremely bad. She watched the other tables fill up. A group of soldiers, freed from the boundaries of the fort for the night, came in a wave of Sixth Cavalry blue. None stopped at Celia's table.

"Guess they know better," Farley muttered.

Madam Agnes came out of her lair in the back of the building and surveyed her domain. Her snaky eyebrows crawled together. Celia looked around her for a friendly face. She smiled at a cowboy who used to play at her table. His lips quivered uncertainly, but he bellied up to the bar instead of coming over to play.

It was as if there was an invisible circle around Celia's table, and the men were afraid to cross the line. Glidinghawk was over by the poker table, sweeping. His coal black eyes were on her, but his face registered a false stupidity.

The tempo of the night increased—except at Celia's table. Celia saw Nellie Vernon leave with her first customer and then return. The faro bank next to Celia's raked in the chips on a hot betting streak. Big Lil was dancing with a bony man half her size. Major Newcomb took his accustomed place at the bar and chatted with Madam Agnes.

Celia tapped her foot impatiently. Standing and waiting made her aware of how hard dealing was on the feet. Simmons skirted her table and stepped up, exhaling a fetid breath as he placed a chip on the deuce.

"I think you and me have to talk," he said. His checked suit was the least obnoxious thing about him. "You might just like to buy a little of what I have."

Celia dealt the cards. He lost, but it was a small satisfaction to her. "I don't think you have anything I could possibly want," she said.

"Yeah?" Simmons said. "How about silence? I'll walk you home after work—unless you want me to sell my information to the major."

He sidled away. Celia thought of what Landrum had told her a lifetime ago, about the snakes in town being harder to spot. She knew who some of them were now. Simmons was one. All she needed on top of her military shadow was a blackmailer haunting her.

Of course, if she didn't get some play soon, the matter would be out of her hands. Her job at the Brazos would be over and that would leave her totally out of the picture. She wanted to be here. She had the feeling that the answer to who murdered Black Jack—and the other men—revolved around the Brazos Club.

She had been standing for two hours with one small play. Where were the men who flirted and joked with her? Where were the men who would just as soon lose at her table as buy a woman?

Celia knew she looked worn and drawn, but surely that was not driving her players away. Was it the rumors, or the military tail, or Simmons—or all blasted three? She had to believe that the men lacked courage. They could not think she was a murderer. The murders had started before she had even arrived in town.

Madam Agnes finally waddled over. A hush fell on the tables she passed. Her wattles quivered as she stood before Celia, gloating. "If your table doesn't make money tonight, you are finished here."

"I've made a lot of money for the Brazos Club," Celia protested. "This is just an off night . . . because of what happened."

"I don't run any charities." Agnes' gold teeth gleamed when she grimaced. "Maybe, though, you could still make money in one of the pigpens. You want to, let me know."

Celia was about to make another grave error by telling Madam Agnes what she thought of the suggestion, when she saw Davis walk in the door with a group of revelers. There were a few hunters and hiders in the group, and some hangers-on who Celia had seen around town. They all seemed in good spirits—whether Squirrel or Old Overholt, Celia could not tell.

"Come'n boys," Landrum slurred, "let's buck the tiger with the little lady. I'll buy the drinks."

The spell was broken.

Bets were placed, and the men who had been holding back joined in with Davis' group. Celia stacked her decks with pairs and used every other device in the dealer's trade to make money for the house. Sneaky Pete—fingers sliding beads up and down the spindles of the case—and Farley had trouble keeping bets straight. Celia had never dealt faster, better or more dishonestly in her life.

On orders from Major Newcomb, Fox took a seat by Celia's table and stared at her. She ignored him, and his presence no longer deterred the men. Davis had managed to whip them up to a gambling frenzy.

Between deals, she tried to talk to him.

"Hey hider, thanks for bringing your pals."

The scar across Landrum's cheek whitened, a sign of the tension he was under. "Anything for you, Red. I think someone around here was setting you up. Sorry about your gambling man."

Celia blinked rapidly and laughed up at another bettor. "You lucky enough tonight to call the last turn?" The words were right but her voice was husky. Davis' unexpected sympathy had stirred up the sorrow—and she would just as soon stay angry.

"I'll get them, hider, I'll get them," she chanted between gambling jargon. Davis nodded. He had seen death change boys into men with vengeance in their hearts. He saw the same change in Celia. He could not point to the difference, but it was there.

"You do that, Red," he said.

Later, he split off from the group he had brought in. Celia knew he could not hang around her too closely or too long, but she was sorry to see him go. She knew that she would have to handle the rest of the night alone.

"Your tally came out okay," Samuel announced, seating himself so close to Celia that she could smell his sweat. For an indoor man, he sweated a lot, but it was not the clean odor of honest outdoor sweat. It was stale and sickly smelling.

"Good. I'll be seeing you tomorrow night, then."

She rose to leave. Sam's moist hand grabbed her arm. "I'll buy you a decent drink."

"And keep my friends here up?" Celia laughed, motioning her head at Fox, sitting with Newcomb, further down the bar.

Samuel's chuckle was nasty. "You sure have gotten popular. Why, I believe that guy is going to watch every move you make. You going to lead them to the money?"

"If Black Jack left any, it certainly wasn't to me," Celia flared. "Or I wouldn't be working here. Why don't you ask Nellie where the money is? She had her hooks into him."

Samuel's only answer was a pat square on her rump. Celia highly resented it. As she left through the side door, she saw Fox scurry off his bar stool. He had just ordered a fresh drink.

The night air was damp. Celia leaned against the building and reached under her skirt. She had loaded her derringer before coming to work. She wanted it handy now. Simmons was nowhere in sight. She was going straight back to the hotel—and God help anyone who got in her way.

She supposed Fox would be pussyfooting after her.

The Flats were closing in around her. She could hardly remember how glittering and bright the place had seemed the night Black Jack introduced her to it. Now, she read death in the beckoning lights and in the embrace of the women who plied their trade here.

She thought she heard footsteps several paces behind her. Fox, she thought. She hurried ahead, ducked into a doorway, and waited. It was the lieutenant. He walked by, frantic, and went beyond her, peering into alleys and up ahead at the lights from the hotel.

Celia felt a brief thrill of triumph. Fox was, of course, supposed to be on her side, but events had become too complicated. She knew she could not trust him. Privately, she had thought he was a pantywaist from the first moment she had met him. Further meetings had only reinforced her opinion.

She stayed in the doorway long enough to give Fox heart palpitations. Maybe this was a silly game. She would be better off if Fox knew she went back to the hotel, so he could report it. But dammit all, it felt good to give him the slip.

He had made it to the hotel and was doubling back, craning his neck from one shadow to another, muddying his boots. He looked like a rat confronting a maze—and Celia knew she was the cheese.

When he ducked into an alley half a block up, perhaps attracted by the sounds of a couple bargaining over the woman's price, Celia saw her chance. She would casually

156

stroll on, so that when Fox returned to the main street, she would be innocently walking by him. Maybe she would even say good evening. She could not wait to see the expression on his face.

Her mind was on the small game she was playing. She was totally unprepared for the strong arms that grabbed her and pulled her away. She opened her mouth to cry out, but it was too late.

One of Simmons' large hands was over her mouth. He gripped her from behind. His other fist dug into her ribcage and breasts. She struggled and kicked against him, but he was a powerful man. She heard and smelled his wheezing breath whistling by her ear. It was a feral, rotten smell.

"Just keep quiet," he warned. "I told you I wanted to talk to you."

With his fingers digging into her face and covering her mouth, there was no way Celia could reply. Her arms were pinned to her side. Underneath the shawl she carried, she could feel the warm metal of her derringer.

"I seen you before, Red. Remember the trail? Them friends of yours killed the fellow I was riding with and ran me off, but not before I got a look at you, with that red hair of yours streaming down your back."

"Mmm . . . mmmm!"

"You got something to say, huh? Well, you feel this blade, right here? Don't want no loud noises now, do we? But if you try to yell for help, I'll run this knife right through you. You understand?"

Celia bobbed her head.

He kept talking as the fury she had felt since Black Jack's death rose in her. Her mind was speeding along. If he took away the fingers jamming into her mouth, she might be able to catch him off balance. She tensed her muscles, waiting. She wished Fox would show up.

"So I figure, there's some in town would be mighty interested in a woman who rides with two men. Two rough men, handy with guns. Yup, they'd be mighty interested. But before I can sell that little piece of information, I find the woman has killed a rich gambler. So, the way I figure, she'll pay a little more to keep my mouth shut."

"Mmmmm . . . mmmm."

"So you just let me know what it's worth to you, and you and me can go find that money you stashed. Who knows, maybe you and me can make this more than business."

He thrust his hips forward and Celia felt his hardness digging into her buttocks. It was the final insult. She was sure she felt the blade of his knife against her side, though she could not see it. Suddenly, she did not care if he killed her. She was past reason. She only wanted his slimy hands and body away from her.

She rubbed backwards against him.

He released her mouth so she could answer him.

For a split second, he was off balance. Celia ducked and whirled, smashing forward into his belly, pulling the trigger on her derringer. His eyes opened wide and he slammed back, arms thrown wide, one hand clutching out to her.

The shot echoed in the distance.

It had traveled upward, pierced a lung and smashed into his heart. Celia used to think death by gunshot was instantaneous. She had been wrong.

Simmons' fingers clenched and unclenched spasmodically as a small, dull-bladed knife with a sharp point fell to the muddied earth. It was so small, not deadly looking at all.

A sigh bubbling with pink saliva escaped his lips.

His eyes rolled upward into his head so that the whites and pupils showed like eggs that had been boiled too long. A harsh rattle rose in his chest. It was his last gasp.

CHAPTER SIXTEEN

Fox was the first one to reach them.

Celia was standing over Simmons' prone body, holding her shawl. There was a big, black, smoking hole burned right through it. She turned to Fox, dazed. "He attacked me," she said. "He was going to hurt me."

Fox skittered over to her right. Celia realized she was pointing her weapon right at him as she turned. She dropped her gun hand and let everything fall—shawl, derringer, the small handbag she carried.

Fox knelt over the man, checking for any signs of life. He listened for the man's breath and felt for a pulse. He could not seem to believe that the man was dead. Fox was in as much of a daze as Celia. He looked up at her and said accusingly, "You killed him."

"He knew who I was, and he attacked me."

Fox stared at her. "You really are a killer, aren't you?" Celia didn't bother to answer. There was no answer. She could tell that Fox would be a big help to her if she needed him. She found herself wishing Landrum were there.

The shot had attracted several other men, who peered around the corner and moved on. Fox saw some soldiers among them and ordered, "Over here."

They tried to fade into the shadows, but Fox repeated his order. Two older enlisted men stepped forward. Their eyes were bloodshot from a night of carousing, but they managed to salute the second lieutenant.

"I want you to stay here and guard this woman," Fox told them. "I will be back with Major Newcomb."

For the second time in as many days, the undertaker was called out. The dead man carried no identification. Simmons was probably an alias. As Celia had suspected, he had carried a six-shooter in his waistband. From the way it was secured, it was clear that he had not intended to use it on Celia.

The knife was a joke. "This wouldn't even slice buffalo steak," the major said. "You are in serious trouble, Miss Burnett."

"I can explain," Celia said. "I had no way of knowing it was not a lethal weapon. Let me tell you. . . ."

"I am going to give you the opportunity to explain," the major said. "You will come with me. Madam Agnes has a room I can use to interrogate you."

Fox gave her a smug grin. It was less smug when the major ordered, "I want you to go back to the fort. I need to handle this alone."

Celia found herself upstairs at the Brazos Club in a bedroom, alone with Newcomb. She had never seen this part of the club. It was adjacent to the rooms used by Madam Agnes' top girls.

The room was large and plain, with a big bed in the center of it. A crystal chandelier glittered overhead. Celia had often wondered about seeing the major so frequently in the Flats late at night. This appeared to be his second, off-base headquarters.

The simple furnishings were masculine. A large mahogany wardrobe, a dresser, a veneer desk and several chairs. Had it been Celia's place to ask the questions, she knew several she wanted answers to. The main thing she wondered about was just how tightly Major Newcomb was tied to the workings of the Brazos Club.

But Celia had just gunned down a man. She was also the prime suspect in Black Jack's death and in the theft of his fortune. At the moment, she had no rights.

She faced the major silently.

"Sit down," he barked. "I'm not going to string you up. Go ahead. Sit."

She did, in the armchair under the light. The major was strangely agitated. He hovered over her like a bird of prey, deciding where her vulnerable points were. Finally, he took the chair opposite her, threading his fingers together and knitting his brow in concentration.

"You never saw that man before?" he asked.

Celia paused. She could not very well tell him that Simmons had been traveling with a bunch of horse thieves several months back. Not unless she was ready to pull out the papers identifying her as an undercover agent for the army—and that she would only do as a last resort.

"I want some answers," Newcomb demanded.

"I saw him earlier at the club, when I was dealing, Major Newcomb," Celia said. That much was true.

"And he attacked you without provocation?"

"Yes, Major Newcomb."

"You may call me Bernard," the major said. "After all, I think we should be friends."

This tact surprised Celia and it showed. Her jaw

163

dropped open. Something was going on here that she was not quite grasping. She nodded, trying to buy time.

"Oh, I surprised you, did I?" His voice became deep and throaty. "Oh, Celia, I have had my eye on you, and tonight was good. I could not have planned it better. A stranger, a murderous stranger, comes along and simplifies everything," he mused.

"I don't understand, Major . . . I mean, Bernard."

"You will," he promised.

He rose to answer a knock at the door to the bedroom and returned with a bottle of imported wine. He sat and poured, placing a glass in her hand. Stunned, Celia drank. He did not, but he smiled at her encouragingly.

Was it possible that the major was now working with her team on the murders, Celia wondered. He did not look stern now. He seemed to want to protect her.

An enraptured look crossed his face. He made a church and steeple with his hands, smiling softly at his handiwork. "You didn't think I would let them punish you for Black Jack's murder, did you?"

"They couldn't. I mean, I know I am under suspicion because of that hotel clerk, but surely once the federal marshal is called in, I can explain everything to him. The murders in the Flats started long before I arrived."

The major chuckled. It was friendly and frightening at the same time, like the first cackle of insanity. "No federal marshals here, my dear. The citizens trust me to keep their little town safe. You must know that the army post *is* the town. Or rather, the town exists because of the post. And who has more power? Well . . . I am diverging from the point."

"And just what is the point?"

"You defended yourself beautifully tonight, Celia.

You killed the man who murdered your lover."

It was so simple that it was breathtaking.

Celia was in the clear. By shifting a few facts, the major solved the crime. And who knows—Simmons might have been responsible for Black Jack's death. Celia would not have to reveal herself as an army operative. The case was closed.

It was so neat.

"It is brilliant, isn't it?" Newcomb congratulated himself, toasting. "We can all get on with our lives. In the morning, I will make the announcements . . . that is, if you agree?"

A languor had stolen over her. Celia's limbs felt weak and unable to support her. Her will was bending to his, and it was so easy to sink into his power. And why not, when he was trying to save her reputation while enhancing his own?

Strange, she thought, that she was used to hard whiskey and this wine was affecting her so much. Newcomb poured her another glass. She raised it to her lips and it felt heavy as a rock. Her hand separated from the rest of her body. She was numb and tingling at the same time.

Shadows flickered across the major's face as it loomed larger and closer. His thin lips pressed into her softer ones. Feebly, she turned her face away, but he was all over her, smothering her, his mouth hard and unyielding.

"I told you I had my eye on you. We are in this together now. Don't fight me."

Her mind spun like the cylinder of an unloaded gun, coming up empty. Did he mean all of them, in this together? Did he include himself, along with Landrum, Glidinghawk and Fox, working for Amos Powell?

Even if he was on her side, Celia did not want him. Was he assuming that she was free, now that Black Jack was dead? Did he think she wanted him? It was an effort to talk, but she tried.

"But I don't love you," she said. She thought she spoke loudly, but her voice seemed to be coming from very far away.

He brayed. She was so naive. He picked her up like a piece of furniture that did not fit that corner of the room. He dropped her across his wide bed, laughing without humor.

"Love? Who said anything about love? I want you and I'm going to have you. Unless you want to play it the other way. If those vigilantes get worked up, you'll probably be hanged for murder."

The worst thing was that Celia could see what was happening to her, could feel it, but everything seemed to be at a great distance, as if she were watching someone else. She watched as he tore the dress from her weakened body and flung it to the floor, watched as he stripped his uniform off, hanging it reverently in the wardrobe, with every crease just so. In a way, Celia admired his excessive neatness; the drugged wine had set her mind free into a world where this whole thing made perfect sense.

He had come up with a plan as neat as his uniform, and it seemed only natural that their coupling was part of it. This was a rough game, and it was his deal.

Celia did not know how long it lasted. She thought she sobbed and cried out. When it was over, she closed her eyes and tried to make the world go away. Stars whirled around inside her eyelids, but they were not the bright scattershot stars of the plains. They were the points of light on an overhead chandelier, crystal bright and brittle.

She was alone when she awoke. At first, she could not remember what had happened. As it came back to her, she sank back under the covers, wishing she could hide forever.

Celia felt unclean.

Though she had not invited the major's advances, somehow their coupling seemed to be her fault. She felt like she was no better than the women who sold themselves.

They had, she recalled, made a deal. Now she was supposed to be free—but free from what? She had trouble thinking. She had not killed Black Jack.

Then the image of Simmons falling away from her surfaced. She stared down at the finger that had pulled the trigger. She had killed. Last night had been her punishment.

Her head felt strange and hazy. Perhaps she had too much to drink and did, indeed, lead the major on. Maybe she was going crazy.

Or maybe she was not crazy, but this whole thing was. She only knew that she felt dirty and ashamed. She lay still for a long time. Shafts of sunlight refracted on the crystal droplets of the overhead light.

She wanted to die.

She forced herself to get up. Her dress was ripped across the bodice. She put it on anyway. There was a small mirror above the bureau and she looked at the reflection of her face for a long time. It was like looking at the face of a stranger.

Celia did not like what she saw. The lines under her eyes were dark and harsh. The downward cast to her face made her look old and defeated. She looked far worse than any women from the pigpens she had met on the street.

How could she explain to Davis and Glidinghawk? Should she tell them and bear her shame? Or did they already know? What was she supposed to do now?

Somehow, she would have to force herself to go on. She would go back to the Vagabond Hotel, to her own room. She would go to work tonight as if nothing had happened.

Celia would do her job and stay as far away from the major as she could. Whatever had really happened last night, she knew she did not want a repeat performance.

The soft knock on the door cut into her morbid reverie. She opened it cautiously. She could not have been more surprised. She found herself staring at the picket-fence overbite of Annie Downey. Suds Row Annie.

"Miss Celia, let me in," the ugly woman said. She carried several dresses and lengths of cloth with her. "Hurry, please, and be quiet," Annie whispered.

Celia stepped back as she entered and shut the door. "What are you doing here? What is it?"

"I heard about last night. I figured you'd be here, and I have something for you. I haven't forgotten how you helped me find a room in town and get me some business. They don't notice my comings and goings around here. I had some fittings to do. Here, I figured you'd be needing this."

Annie handed Celia a dress, one she had ordered several weeks before. It was a proper street dress, one Celia figured she might use after her job in the saloon was over.

"Thank you," Celia said, taking it. She had been wondering how she was going to walk through the Flats in her torn garment without attracting attention. "How did you know I'd need this?"

Annie sucked her lips over her prominent teeth. "I know about the major more than I let on. He's a bad one, I can tell you. When talk was he took you away for questioning, I knew there was more to it. I could tell you stories, I could. . . ."

Celia quickly peeled her torn dress off and put on the decent one. She wanted to hear everything Annie knew, but this was neither the time nor the place for it.

"Can we talk later?" she asked. "I think we'd both better get out of here now."

Annie shrugged, clucking her tongue. "If you want." She took Celia's defiled dress in her hands. "You want me to take this and mend it for you?"

"No!" Celia said. "Please throw it away for me. I never want to see it again."

Celia started to follow the older woman out of the bedroom, but Annie stopped her. "You have been my friend," Annie said, "but there's no sense letting on to the likes of them around here."

So ten minutes after Annie left, Celia squared her shoulders and marched down the stairs alone. Her cheeks flamed when she passed Samuel Wallace on the stairs. He gave her a lecherous leer along with a knowing wink.

She had never been so glad to escape a place as she was

169

the building that housed the Brazos Club. She dreaded returning for her nightly shift. She was beginning to be eager for this whole mission to be over.

She couldn't help wondering how many more people would die before it was finished. She no longer had confidence that she wouldn't be one of them.

CHAPTER SEVENTEEN

"It ain't Saturday," the clerk mumbled sullenly. He shuffled and looked down at the floor. By now, the Flats were buzzing with the news that the man Celia shot was responsible for the murders in the Flats. She was a heroine, not a suspect.

Celia was sore and bruised. She had ordered the room clerk—the same mousey clerk who had accused her of sneaking into Black Jack's room the night he was murdered—to prepare a bath for her.

"I don't give a damn what day it is," Celia said. "I want some hot water right now. I will expect my bath to be ready in twenty minutes."

"Well, this time of year, ain't had no complaints about cold water. But if you're going to get huffy, I could get you some heated; fire will take about an hour, hauling it and so on, say another half—"

"Do it," Celia ordered.

"And it'll cost extra, since this ain't a Saturday."

Celia's look withered him, but he was used to contempt. What he wasn't used to—from a woman—was the bulge in her small handbag. It sure looked like her small derringer, the one she was so handy with the night before. And, the clerk knew, she had reason to be mighty sore with him.

Her meaning was clear, but still she added, "Forty-five minutes, unless you want a taste of what Simmons got."

"Yes, m'am!"

Her bath was ready with five minutes to spare. Celia was not used to bullying people, but getting a little of her own back with the clerk had been satisfying.

She wished she still had her gun. It had been confiscated by the major last night. The bulge in her handbag, unfortunately, was a small prayer missal. She hoped to find a few appropriate words to say over Black Jack's grave.

She sank back in the galvanized tub—the water was lukewarm, but not cool enough to make a fuss over—and scrubbed until her skin felt raw. Between her legs, she ached dully. She attacked herself with strong lye soap, wondering if she would ever feel clean again.

A bang on the door startled her. "Hey lady, I get that water when you're through. Give a shout, will you?"

She should have figured the shifty clerk would find some way to profit from having to arrange a bath during the week. Then she shrugged. If some cowboy wanted to pay for her used bathwater, that was his problem.

But when the door opened a crack, she started to swear—then she saw Suds Row Annie's tear-filled eyes peek into the room.

"Annie, what are you doing here? What's wrong? Stop crying."

"It's . . . oh, I know you have trouble enough, but it's Big Lil. I hope you can help."

The older woman was ugly enough without her face blotched with tears. Her nose was red, too. She was

172

usually stoic and uncomplaining, well grounded in common sense. A little timid, she had once told Celia that she wanted only to fit into life "without no man, and without no troubles."

"Tell me what it is, and what I can do," Celia said. She had been surprised when Annie came to her rescue earlier, and she was even more amazed that Annie would turn to her now. Both Celia and Big Lil had helped Annie, but neither had expected doglike devotion from her.

"Madam Agnes kicked Lil out of the Brazos Club, made her go work the pigpen. Arlene's, down by the river bottom. Took her down there and left her. Big Lil kicked up a storm, crying and carrying on. She's drunk enough laudanum to kill a grown man, and she won't stop."

Celia had heard about Arlene's. It was about as far down as a woman could go, the dregs of the profession. The women there were disease-ridden, alcoholic and rough. "Why didn't Big Lil refuse? There are a lot of places she could work. Her customers like her."

"You don't understand, do you?" Annie said. "Madam Agnes don't just run girls and work them, she owns them, same as she owns all the whorehouses in town. She gets a woman who's in trouble somewhere else, trouble with the law, and bails them out, promises nice work in a swell joint."

Celia was following. She had always known that Madam Agnes had iron control over her girls, but she had not imagined it was this bad. Celia had to find out if this was a product of Annie's imagination, or truth.

The door rattled again. "You going to be outta there today?" the cowboy whined. "I paid for my bath time."

"Yes," Celia returned, "but you can tell that little man downstairs I'm gunning for him after this."

173

Annie's protruding eyes widened.

Celia got out of the tub and dried herself, whispering to Annie, "I would think Lil could just leave town, maybe not go back where she came from, but go somewhere. . . ."

"There's one stage out of town, you know that. Big Lil, like the rest of them, ends up owing more to Samuel and the madam than she earns. And the major, he puts the word out a woman has a bad debt, who's going to help her?"

"I am," Celia said decisively. "Let me get dressed and we'll go down to Arlene's pigpen and see about this."

The two women debated about being seen together, but Annie's anger and concern for Big Lil had wiped away her timid reserve.

"I reckon I always would have been in trouble with that Brazos Club gang, Major Newcomb included," Annie sniffed, "except they think some no-account as ugly as I am ain't worth bothering about."

So they walked side by side to the outskirts of town, where Arlene operated her pigpen. A pie-eyed soldier whistled at Celia and offered, "Sugar, I'll take you in an Eastern minute"—everybody knew how those back-east people rushed—"if you can ditch that sowbelly you're with."

Celia did not bother to reply.

The main part of the Flats, where the fancy drink, dance and gambling halls were located, was no garden paradise, but it wasn't bad. Boardwalks, lighted streets at night and hasty paint jobs on the false fronts gave it a carnival air.

Further on, the rutted alleys and shacks stank of unwashed bodies and poor sanitation. Slop pails were emptied into the ditches. A huge rat scurried directly across Celia's path.

The women staring out of the shacks were more than likely fifteen, but most of them looked fifty. Their eyes were sunken hollows, without hope. Grogshops were the only businesses, besides the houses of prostitution, that were active here.

Annie shivered. "If I wasn't handy with a needle and thread, if you and Big Lil didn't help, I would have ended up here. I feel like I'm walking over my own grave."

Celia nodded. There was a time when she had looked down on the women of easy virtue, believing what she had been taught, that they took the easy way out. Now, she knew there was nothing easy about their lives.

A young girl with the ravaged face of an old crone brushed by Celia and grabbed at her handbag. Celia whirled around and knocked the thief on the head with it. Like the rat, the girl scampered out of sight.

They stood outside Arlene's. They could hear a caterwauling from deep in the bowels of the crib. Celia had heard Big Lil's deep, hearty tones in flesh-shaking laughter; this sound was familiar, but gut-wrenching. It was Big Lil, wailing out her agony.

Celia stepped through the threshold. The place was unpainted board, hastily hammered together, with about twenty-five cubicles opening on a dimly lit hallway. In the front, at a three-legged table, sat a frowsy blond in a stained dress. Arlene.

"We are here to see Big Lil," Celia announced.

"Hm. Thought maybe you was applying for a job. You look a little uppity, the kind needs the starch whipped outa them, but your friend here would do just fine, if she kept her mouth shut. What a set of chompers."

Working girls with sleep in their eyes peered out of their cubicles with indifferent hostility. It was afternoon, but the cribs did not get busy until night mercifully hid and transformed the shabby surroundings. Nothing could mask the smell, however.

"I hear my friend back there and I'm going to go speak to her," Celia said. Arlene was now standing directly in her path, blocking the way. She was unsteady on her feet.

"You two got a thing going?" she challenged, slurring her words. "Ho, ho, wait till Madam Agnes hears about this. That fancy, fat tub of lard, moaning her life away has woman friends. How much you gonna pay for Big Lil's time? You want to see her, I collect."

Gritting her teeth, Celia tossed a five-dollar gold piece on Arlene's table and marched down the planked corridor with Suds Row Annie at her heels. Their footsteps echoed tinnily on the cheap floorboards.

Big Lil was in the last cubicle, guarded by a woman, dressed in pants, who looked more like a man. A brown fuzz covered the woman's upper lip and she looked tougher than a hardcase. She scowled at Celia and Annie.

Behind her, they could see their friend lying across her cot and moaning. She heaved to her right, and an empty bottle of laudanum clattered to the floor. Her eyes ricocheted in their direction, but she did not see them. She keened and turned her head to the wall, her black sausage curls bouncing.

"I'm Emma and I keep the girls in line," the manly woman said. "You two joining us, or just here for a visit? This woman," Emma punctuated her remark by spitting, "is nothing but trouble, but I got my orders. What the hell you want?"

"I paid for Big Lil's time," Celia said. "Annie and I

want to talk to her. Alone."

"I'll just see about that," Emma said, wiping her faint mustache with the back of her hand.

"You do that," Celia said. "Check with Arlene. She took my money."

Emma grunted and left, striding like a bowlegged man. Celia was shocked by the masculine enforcer, but Annie just shrugged, as if this was what she expected at a place like Arlene's. Annie, Celia was finding, was far more knowledgeable about the rough side of life than she was.

Now, the gap-toothed woman knelt by Lil's side and shook her. "Big Lil, it's Annie and Celia. Pull yourself together. Maybe we can do somethin'."

Lil was pretty far gone, but she turned her eyes away from the wall. "It's too late," she said, mumbling to herself. "They got me here and the only way I'll ever get out is in a coffin. This is where it ends."

Annie turned to Celia. "Get some water. One of the girls ought to have a pitcher. Quick."

Celia wished she could fade into the woodwork. She had to force herself back into the hall, where Emma was chatting with Arlene. They were looking out the front door and did not see her.

Celia poked her head into an adjoining room and spotted a pitcher. The woman in there was asleep or passed out on her bed. Celia grabbed the water and hurried back to Annie, who took it and dumped it on Big Lil's head.

The plump woman came up spluttering. The pupils of her eyes were small pinpoints, but they no longer stared at nothing. At last, she seemed to recognize them.

"That's it," Annie encouraged. For such a spectacularly ugly woman, her voice now sounded like silk,

177

smooth and comforting. "Sit up and listen."

"What for?" Big Lil said, straining with the effort of sitting upright. Annie put an arm around her shoulder and helped her. "Get into one of these pigpens, nobody can help."

"We can try. Oh, Lil, what hold do they have on you? There's plenty of decent places that would have you. . . ." Celia blinked rapidly.

Lil shook her head hopelessly. Her black hair hung in wet strands that clung to her rounded cheeks. Her rouge and mascara streaked her face, the face of an unhappy clown.

"I might as well tell you. Annie knows how it is with me. A long ways back, when I was working 'round Fort Stanton, I killed a soldier. He was a customer, a man I never seen before. He got rough and I hit him over the head with a chair. He died."

"So?" Celia said. Fear raced through her. This story sounded too much like her own. A threat, a killing, and entrapment. "It was self-defense; surely you could prove that?"

"In an army town?" Big Lil said. "The army is the law in them places. Major Newcomb was there then, and he saved me, told me he could get me out of town to work for a madam at a swell place in Fort Griffin. That's how I ended up at the Brazos Club, with a murder hanging over my head."

Celia knew the rest. Big Lil worked at the club, but Samuel Wallace and the madam charged room rent and board. Big Lil had ended up owing them. And she was, in a way, their slave. Behind it all was Major Newcomb, upright, law-abiding Major Newcomb.

"Are you sure the man you hit died?" Celia asked.

178

"What if you only knocked him out?" She was remembering the townsman Glidinghawk had knocked out, and how dead he had looked.

Glidinghawk . . . maybe he would know how to get Big Lil out of this mess. Davis, too, would have some ideas, if only she could get word to them.

"Hah! Had to be deader than a doornail," Big Lil snorted—but a shadow of doubt had crept in. "He had a big lump on his head when the major carried him out. . . ."

"Big Lil, you have to sober up and get that laudanum out of your blood."

Lil moaned, "I'm not sure but I'd as soon lay down and die, now't I'm here. There's no way out."

"Yes, there is," Celia said. She hoped she was not lying. "Something about the major and Madam Agnes and the whole setup stinks worse than this pigpen . . . and I know a few people who are about to get to the bottom of it."

Big Lil looked at her, really looked at her. Celia could not say more. Her thoughts were whirling. She could not risk Emma and Arlene listening in. Chances were they were already on the other side of the thin door.

She dropped her voice to a whisper. "You have to trust me. I'm going to figure a way to get you out of here."

"Emma is guarding me," Big Lil said. "Not that I'd run, since I don't have any place to go. . . ."

"You will have," Celia promised. "Annie and I have to go now. I can't tell you just what will happen, but you have to straighten up, to be ready. Can you do that?"

"I'll try," Lil promised.

"Don't let them know it," Celia cautioned. "Keep carrying on the way you have, but get ready to move. Do you own a weapon?"

"No. I wouldn't be able to use one if I had it. After I killed a man with a chair, I don't want no weapons in my life. All I wanted was to do good and forget it."

"Someday soon, I think you'll be able to," Celia said with more conviction than she felt.

As they were leaving, Arlene asked, "You got what you paid for? You have a good time?"

Celia shook her head bitterly. "She's never going to leave here, is she? You have her right where you want her, flat on her back."

"Ho, ho," Arlene taunted, "you think you can save somebody with your high and mighty words. When a woman's sunk this low, nobody cares any more. She don't even care. You might not believe it, but I worked them fancy places once. See what it got me."

"Shut your mouth," Emma warned.

Arlene took another long pull from her bottle. "Just you wait, Miss Fancy-Gambling-Lady. One of these days, you're going to end up just like me . . . and it might be sooner than you think."

Remembering how she had lain back dully while Major Newcomb used her, Celia walked more quickly, trying to flee the harsh laughter that followed her.

"Slow down," Annie begged, taking quick, trotting steps to keep up with Celia. "We're going about as fast as the news we've been there. What do we do now?"

That, Celia realized, was the biggest question of all. She knew she would try to work tonight. She knew she had to get Glidinghawk to help Big Lil. She knew she had to avoid any further advances from the major.

She just didn't know how.

At that moment, when she should have been worrying about Annie Downey, Celia was caught up in fear for her own safety. She knew everything was about to blow up, and she was caught squarely in the middle.

Celia wanted to run, but like Big Lil, she didn't know where to run to. She desperately needed to talk to the other members of her team.

Before they parted, she told Annie, "I'll work something out. You go on home and stay there. If an Indian shows up, tell him everything we learned today, about Big Lil and the so-called murder and especially about the major. Will you do that?"

Annie replied darkly, "If they don't get to me first."

CHAPTER EIGHTEEN

Time was running out for all of them, including
Lieutenant Colonel Amos Powell back at Fort Leavenworth, as the month of June came to an end.

Communications between the Department of Texas
and the Territorial Command in Kansas were slower than
usual. The last mail run from Fort Griffin had been held
up by a roving band of Kiowas. The Plains Indians were
getting downright civilized, taking money and papers
instead of scalps.

Amos sighed. Perhaps he had missed a message from
his agents. Next mission—if there was a next mission,
Amos reminded himself—he would work out a code for
telegram messages, so Landrum Davis could contact him
quickly and directly, instead of going through Fox.

Second Lieutenant Preston Kirkwood Fox was hopeless. When Amos had failed to reply to Fox's first
report—the one relating that he had been punched out
by Davis—he had issued a second one, aggravating an
already dicey security situation. If that message had fallen under the wrong eyes, Powell's Army would have
been blown wide open. It had cost Amos many sleepless
nights.

To: Lt. Col. Amos Powell, Adj. Gen.
Fort Leavenworth Territorial Command
Kansas

Since I received no updated orders granting the
autonomous powers I requested for myself and one
Major Newcomb, as per my communique of
April 15 of this year, an oversight I trust you will
remedy, I have exercised the discipline befitting a
West Point officer and maintained the status quo as
outlined in your orders prior to this mission.

To my chagrin, this leaves me as a distant and
powerless observer, a situation it is imperative you
remedy forthwith. Sir, I implore you, the latest
indignities committed by the undercover operatives, code names *A, B,* and *C,* leave neither of us
with any other choice but to take control.

First, Operative *A* had the audacity to openly show
herself at the fort and, as if this were not improper
enough, in view of the fact that she has sunk to the
lowest level of frontier society, she openly flirted
with Major Newcomb, no doubt trying to sway him
for her nefarious purposes—a statement of great
import, in view of the subsequent events.

I can only speculate herewith and let you draw your
own conclusions. Operative *A* had been carrying on
what embarrasses me to refer to as a torrid affair
with the cardsharper known as Black Jack. What
dark and evil passions this stirred up in her I can
only guess, but the gambler was found in his room

murdered and mutilated in a manner so indelicate I shall not detail it here. It was established by the hotel clerk that Operative *A* had obtained the key to his room. Suspicion for the murder rested squarely on her shoulders, as an accessory if not the actual perpetrator. Major Newcomb, who has taken it upon himself to be responsible for whatever law and order exists in this prurient hellhole, astutely stated this fact.

Immediately following this contretemps, Operative *A* gunned down a man in cold blood. She claimed the man, who called himself Simmons, attacked her in a threatening manner. As if this were not suspicious enough, she exerted her wily charms on Major Newcomb and convinced him that Simmons was the murderer of the Flats. Be that as it may (and far be it from me to question a career army officer of Major Newcomb's caliber), it occurs to me that she is not empowered to kill, and thus has provided sufficient cause for her immediate removal from the employ of the army (and good riddance, I should add, a sentiment I am sure you will join me in).

Meanwhile, Operative *B* continues to be regarded as the lowest of scum, and I shudder to think what a low opinion people would have of the military if his connection with us should come out. Operative *C* is no better, I assure you, and boasts of the money he is making as a hider. He is seen in the lowest pigpens throughout the Flats, supposedly gathering information, but as grown men, sir, I implore you to consider the ramifications of his actions. It would not be going too far to say that he is having a rowdy time at the army's expense.

In conclusion, I await further orders, trusting you will take emergency measures to give me the authority to terminate Operatives *A, B,* and *C* before they should bring further disgrace upon the institution we both hold dear, the U.S. Army.

June 23, 1874   Fox

Wordy bastard, Amos thought. After this mission was over, one way or the other, Amos couldn't wait to get his hands on the lieutenant. Fox would see just who was terminated.

As for the others, Amos had no doubt they were doing their jobs to the best of their abilities. It was a shame Celia Louise Burnett had been forced to kill a man. If she came through this, she would be a seasoned operative, more valuable than ever. The girl had a head on her shoulders, and if she had shot someone, Amos knew damned well she had good reason.

He only hoped Glidinghawk and Davis were able to keep an eye on her. Amos didn't like the idea that she had been forced to cozy up to Major Newcomb.

Amos was not usually given to blasphemous or crude thoughts, but he, too, could be pushed just so far. If Fox wasn't so busy kissing the major's ass, he reflected, the whippersnapper would see that something about Newcomb was not what it seemed.

Amos Powell had pulled the records on Bernard Newcomb. On the surface, it was admirable. Newcomb was stern, disciplined, law-and-order, military—by the book all the way.

Reading between the lines, Amos had found some disquieting facts. One, the major had been transferred from Fort Stanton after overzealous discipline measures had crippled one of the enlisted men under him.

Checking deeper, Amos discovered that several other men under Newcomb's command had been listed as deceased. Causes included a gangrenous wound received in training, viral pneumonia resulting from a drunken debauch, and careless misuse of firearms.

Most curious was a nearly illegible—and illiterate—note written by an army deserter. How this had come into the hands of the Adjutant General's office was anyone's guess, but, fortunately, the army never threw away any scrap of paper. Amos could attest to that: he now had a file cabinet devoted to Fort Griffin and his undercover operatives.

"Mabe this wil git to the army, mabe not. Seein as i'm dyin it don't matter, but i weren't no deserter by my choyce. Major newcom offred me money to get bonged on the head by some hoor an play ded, which I don for him. he almost kilt me instead of paying what he sayed he wood. I hadda run but not afore he hurt me real bad. I'm hold up in the nations now. If yu shood get this, I left a wife behind an my name is john miller and mabe you cood tell her."

But, clear as the picture shaping up Amos' mind was, he needed more than the dying note of a man officially listed as a deserter—and Amos had less than fourteen days left to get some solid facts.

A correspondence from Pee Wee Hurst had arrived the

day before. It was not official, but it was far from encouraging.

Damn the man, Amos thought. Pee Wee and Preston Fox were of the same ilk—as far as Amos was concerned, the greatest weakness of the army. All by the book and West Point, and not an ounce of common horse sense.

Hurst had written in his stilted hand:

"Dear Amos,
    Perhaps it is premature to extend my appreciation, but I soon expect to collect the considerable wager I told you about. . . ."

There was more, but Amos hoped he was above the petty gossip of Washington City, particularly since most of it was both vicious and unfair.

Amos was not an overly religious man—he too often had to play God himself—but he felt if there was any justice in the universe, Hurst, Major Newcomb and that little prig Fox would soon get their comeuppance.

He drummed his fingertips against the hard oak of his desk. Sitting in Fort Leavenworth, there was very little he could do but wait. And that, Amos knew, was the most difficult job of all.

By now, Amos was convinced that even if Major Newcomb was not at the bottom of the criminal acts at Fort Griffin, he was a very vicious man. The kind of man it would be a pleasure to court-martial.

Amos had seen it before, the men who misused their authority and actually enjoyed punishing those under them. Under their veneer of military uprightness lurked an evil beast ready to attack. A beast almost impossible to trap.

CHAPTER NINETEEN

Celia felt the people staring at her as she walked down the street. Every move and sound made her jump. She was known to visit the club during the afternoons; her friendship with Big Lil and the other saloon gals had taken care of that. But this afternoon Big Lil would not be there. And Major Newcomb might.

She would have to brazen it out. Big Lil's life might depend on making contact with Glidinghawk.

Celia's heart thudded loudly in her ears as she strode past the batwing doors into the saloon. As her eyes adjusted to the light, she saw a poker game in progress, several faro tables getting fair play—including the one she would preside over later—and the gaggle of painted women waiting for customers.

Glidinghawk was not in sight.

Neither Samuel nor Madam Agnes was around, but Celia knew she could not trust that situation to last long. Agnes in particular had a way of spying and then sneaking up on her employees when they were least expecting it. The major was, Celia hoped, back at the fort.

Celia took a deep breath. She was tempted to ask the barkeeper for a shot. She needed something to steady her nerves. But she thought better of it. This could be a very long and dangerous night and she would need to be sharp.

"You going to stand there catching flies?" Nellie Vernon challenged from the whores' table. "I have something to say to you, and you'd better get it straight."

Nellie had obviously found out what had happened with Major Newcomb, and she didn't like it one bit. Homely Gertrude and Colored Susan were also sitting there. They looked unusually subdued.

Celia hesitated for a moment. She wanted Glidinghawk to show up. She needed him. She also needed to stall for time, to have a reason for stopping by the club. She sat down at the table facing Nellie.

"I heard what happened to Big Lil, and I wanted to find out if there is anything we can do. . . ."

"I'll bet," Nellie said, sarcastically. Then she leaned toward Celia and hissed in her face, "You stay away from the major, you hear me. I'll tear you open and eat your heart if you don't leave him alone."

Then Celia made a grave mistake.

She tried to reason with Nellie. "I have no interest in Major Newcomb. . . ."

She didn't get a chance to finish.

Nellie tossed a drink in her face. It was not bar tea. It stung Celia's eyes. Instinctively, she reeled back, spluttered, and let fly with her right hand. She slapped the jealous blond smack across her perfectly oval face. The loud slap raised a welt almost as red as Nellie's long fingernails.

Like a bobcat attacking, Nellie's lethal claws raked out. Swiftly, they aimed for Celia's eyes. Celia turned her head just in time, and they grazed her chin instead. Nellie's lips drew back in a snarl as she spit and hissed.

"You no-account hussy, I'll teach you to mess with my man. I'll get you for that. . . ."

All the pent up fears and frustrations of the last several days erupted along with Celia's temper. She was beyond thought. She sprang from her seat and pulled Nellie clear off her chair, fists pounding.

Nellie might look like a porcelain doll of an angel—fallen variety—but she fought like a hellion. She raised her right leg, silken skirts rustling, and kneed Celia squarely in the crotch. Celia grabbed a hank of Nellie's long blond tresses and pulled. Nellie yelped as tears of pain glazed her cold blue eyes.

She turned and bit Celia on the shoulder so hard that she drew blood. They grappled, each trying to get the advantage, locked together in a frenzied dance of hate. Celia broke the deadlock. She rabbit punched the prostitute in the kidneys. Nellie went down, half kneeling on the floor, struggling to get her footing. Celia pounced.

They tumbled to the floor, wrestling.

A crowd of men gathered around, watching avidly. They formed a circle around the two spitfires. They panted, hissed and booed. The only thing better than a good fight was a cat fight between two women, and it didn't come along half often enough.

The women were spectacular in their anger, hair and fists flying, skirts riding up to their thighs. To men who could get hot over inches of exposed ankle, this was a bonanza of flesh and fury.

Celia held her own, but Nellie was a formidable opponent—and she fought dirty. Celia didn't much care about the rules of the game herself. When Nellie got hold of her left breast and twisted, Celia felt for Nellie's chest and gave it a bruising punch.

191

Her hard, balled fist hit something soft, but it wasn't tender flesh. Celia reached for Nellie's neckline and ripped the bodice of her dress clear open to the waist.

"Oh . . . you red-haired bitch!" Nellie panted, drawing her arms protectively around the bosom that had caused so many sleepless nights for the men in the Flats.

But Celia wasn't finished with her. She fingered Nellie's corset and pulled out a wadded up handkerchief, tossing it to the cheering spectators, before digging for another. The strings on Nellie's corset gave way and more padding popped right out.

"I'll be!" One of the men hooted. "Nellie Vernon's flat-chested as a boy!"

Nellie let out a yelp of outrage and doubled her attack. She clamped her teeth together over Celia's right hand, leaving toothmarks behind. She ripped Celia's dress clear off her shoulder. The women kicked, swore and lashed to beat all hell. Spurred on by her public humiliation, Nellie punched Celia in the middle of the nose.

Celia saw stars. When she could focus again, Nellie was on top of her, twisting her arm until Celia thought it would break. She twisted her head around and bit the squawking blond on the upper thigh.

With Nellie off balance, recoiling from the pain, Celia had a momentary advantage and wriggled her way out of Nellie's iron grasp. She half rose, but Nellie recovered and dove for her, bringing her down again.

The air was charged the way it got before a big lightning storm, crackling with menace. Some of the watchers had been rebuffed by Nellie a time or two, when they could not afford her price, so most of the cheering seemed to be for Celia.

192

"I'll kill you, you lily-livered bitch," Nellie spat into Celia's face. She grunted with the effort of speaking and pounding with her fists. One rock-hard hand connected with Celia's jaw. In her fury, Nellie was strong as a man and just as tough.

Celia did not give up, but she was taking quite a beating. She played possum, taking a deep breath, garnering her strength.

Then she twisted and heaved with all her might. She used her whole body, thrusting with her hips. She tossed Nellie off and rolled her sideways, so that her head bounced against the table leg. Colored Susan and Gertrude backed away to safer ground.

Celia jumped forward and straddled Nellie's stomach. She pinned Nellie's arms to her sides, so her bare, flat chest was in full view. A man whistled long and low, but it was not in admiration.

Nellie had come on strong, but she had worn herself out. She was breathing hard, batting her long eyelashes at the crowd, playing for sympathy. She huddled into herself and moaned.

"Please . . . enough . . . let me go," Nellie wailed.

Celia almost bought the act. She softened—until Nellie lashed out again with her long fingernails, slicing Celia's vulnerable cheek. She missed Celia's eyes, but beads of blood popped out against the redhead's white skin like little rubies on velvet.

It was not a wise move.

Celia knew that her opponent would fight until one of them was maimed or killed. She remembered seeing boxers delivering their final blows. Celia stared right at the spot she wanted to hit—the deadly spot just a fraction off center chin—and let loose with an uppercut left punch, putting all her strength behind it.

It hit with a hard crunch of bone on bone. The cheering hit a fevered peak. Celia's doubled-over knuckles cracked.

Nellie's head hit the floor and her eyes rolled white in her head. A strong-smelling man just off the trail grabbed Celia's arm and held it up in the sign for victory. Men yelled and shouted and slapped each other on the back. One wag started a knockout countdown.

Nellie moaned softly and her eyelids fluttered.

Celia figured she'd better get going. Calloused hands reached out to tap her on the back. Hearty voices wheezed and guffawed and congratulated. The swelling sound of victory was heady, but Madam Agnes or Samuel Wallace might show up at any minute.

Colored Susan and Gertrude and several other women knelt by Nellie's side and offered to help her. Nellie rolled her head from side to side. She spluttered, "I'll teach any one of you bitches who messes with my husband. . . ."

The women glanced nervously at Celia, who vainly tried to shake the confusion out of her head.

"That was one swell fight, Red," the blustery cowhand offered. "Buy you a drink?"

Celia stood, a battered warrior in the middle of her well-wishers. She was beginning to feel the scratches and bruises and hoped Nellie felt just as bad when she came to. The very idea of fighting over the attentions of Major Newcomb was a bunch of claptrap. Celia only hoped she could escape before the major showed up. She had never wanted anything to do with him in the first place.

"Maybe white woman need Indian medicine," a familiar voice offered.

"She don't need nothing from a dirty Injun," one of

the saloon regulars said, aiming a kick at Glidinghawk. He sidestepped it and held his ground.

Celia whirled around to him. She felt like falling into his arms. He was dirty and whipped looking, the way he always was around the Brazos Club. He smelled like yesterday's whiskey. His dark eyes, under downcast lids, were clear.

"You got Injun herbs for these?" Celia asked, pointing to the welts on her cheek. She spoke like she was talking to a slow child, the way people always talked to red men.

Lots of people knew about Indian medicine, though they hated to admit it. It was obvious that Indians knew something special about the healing powers of certain plants. And there had been more than one man who spit in Glidinghawk's face whom he had later saved by heathen ways of healing.

"Got good medicine," Glidinghawk repeated stolidly. "You come with me, white lady, and I sell you medicine."

Ah, Celia thought, very good. Greedy, money-grubbing Indians the saloon folks could understand. Celia nodded to Glidinghawk and started to follow him to the side door. No dirty Indian swamper was allowed to use the front door.

A hand touched Celia's shoulder that was laid bare by her ripped dress. "You want me to come with you, Red? Keep an eye on the savage?"

Celia laughed nervously. "I reckon I can handle him," she said. "He's harmless, but I'm not so sure about you."

The men guffawed. Celia had become popular again since she had been cleared of Black Jack's murder and had killed the man who folks were saying was responsible. Now, after besting Nellie Vernon, Celia was more popular than ever.

"You going to be dealing tonight?" A faro player asked.

"You bet," Celia said as she followed Glidinghawk. As soon as they were out of earshot in the alley adjoining the club, Glidinghawk whispered, "One of these days I'm going to show you just how harmless I am."

Celia lowered her voice to a whisper.

"I don't believe anyone is harmless. Not any more. I don't know if they are on to all of us, but Major Newcomb has an unhealthy interest in me. . . ."

Damn, Celia thought. She had to blink rapidly. Glidinghawk touched her hand softly. She did not have to explain.

"You know Annie Downey? Suds Row Annie? She can fill you in on the details. You must talk to her. We have to help Big Lil. . . ."

"Wait a minute," Glidinghawk said. "I know she's been disgraced, farmed out to Arlene's pigpen, but what does that have to do with us?"

"Plenty," Celia said grimly. "I think she can furnish proof that Major Newcomb is not at all what he seems. It goes beyond womanizing, with him. I think he's behind a lot of what's going on here."

That mocking look crossed Glidinghawk's face. "So, you are catching on."

"You knew?" Celia gasped. "You and Landrum knew and you didn't tell me! You. . . ."

"Hold on," Gerald said, grabbing her flailing hands. "We don't have solid proof. And you have done enough fighting for today. We thought you would be safer not knowing what we suspected, and I think we were right."

Celia quieted. What he said made sense. Knowing and

196

pretending she didn't was not as easy as she had thought it would be. At this point, it did not make much difference.

What did make a difference was getting Glidinghawk's word that he and Davis would rescue Big Lil. She knew that the Indian's word could be trusted.

"Will you see what you can do for Big Lil? There's a woman guarding her—dresses like a man and twice as mean. If they ever find out what Lil told me, they might try to kill her."

"I think we can get her," Glidinghawk said. "It'll take two of us. That will leave you alone. Why don't you ride out to that campsite north of town and wait for us. I have a bad feeling about you at the club, especially after what happened."

It was a temptation. She would be safe there. If they got Big Lil out of Arlene's, they might have the proof they needed.

"I can't quit now," Celia said. "We're close to solving the whole Fort Griffin mess, but if anything happens to Lil, we're almost back where we started from. I can manage one more night."

"I don't like it," Glidinghawk repeated. Then, almost to himself, he added, "I'm going to have to tell Fox what we have so far, so he can keep watch over you. You have to have someone. And he has to know, in case none of us makes it. Whoever the killer is, he won't hesitate to kill again."

Celia shivered. Through the drugged fog memory of the night before she recalled the feral gleam of ecstasy on Major Newcomb's face when he was hurting her.

"Yes," she said, "and tell him I don't have a weapon. The major took my derringer last night. Maybe Fox can get a pistol to me. I think I might need one."

"Here, take this," Glidinghawk said, reaching down under his leather trousers for the hunting knife he carried there. "It's all I have with me right now."

Celia took it and slipped it in her handbag. She had never used a knife, except for skinning rabbits. Gutting a man would be different. Even so, she was certain she was up to the task, fueled by her memories.

Memories of Black Jack's body, bloody and violated and very, very dead.

Memories of the major, taking her painfully, thrusting mechanically, stabbing her again and again.

CHAPTER TWENTY

It was too calm at the club.

Celia was worried. Nellie was upstairs recovering from her wounds, the dealer Lucky Jim had told her. Samuel Wallace glared at Celia when she came in, but he staggered into the back room with a full bottle.

Celia was so jittery that her dealing was off. Soldiers, hiders and cowboys won at her faro bank. Word got around, and a crowd of gamblers gathered. Madam Agnes would have had a fit. But Celia couldn't help it. She was nervous as a choirgirl in a whorehouse and her hands hurt like Hades.

Celia began to get suspicious when, after a few hours of steadily losing money for the house, she still hadn't seen or heard from Madam Agnes. She could be cashing in Big Lil's number, Celia thought, not putting anything beyond the capabilities of the madam. After her fight with Nellie, Celia was beginning to wonder whether a woman would have been capable of the Flats slayings, too.

"Ya-hoo! I always knowed you was Lady Luck, Red," a soldier said as Celia paid him out from a diminishing stack of house chips.

Her answering smile was all surface. Her face was lumpy, slightly misshapen, and red welts like war paint decorated her cheeks. She had been in such a hurry, she had worn the same dress she had been wearing the night she broke into Black Jack's room.

"When the bosses find out, you won't be no Lady Luck," Sneaky Pete grumbled. Farley nodded glumly.

Celia's palms were sweaty. It was odd that she wasn't already catching hell. It was just as curious that Newcomb and Fox, who were nightly fixtures at the bar, had not shown up.

Between deals, Celia rubbed her hands inside her pockets to dry them. Her fingers connected with a wadded up piece of paper there.

A strange expression crossed her face and she stood paralyzed. It was the paper she had taken from Black Jack's suit—and forgotten all about when she found the incriminating knife.

In the awful flurry of discovering his body and being accused of his murder, and then the fatal shooting of Simmons, she had forgotten all about it.

Her freckles stood out across her pale face almost as vividly as Nellie's claw marks. She reached for a fresh deck and faltered.

"Red, you better get with it," Farley said. "You going to deal or just stand there?"

"I . . . I . . . you take over," Celia said. "I think I'm having an attack of the vapors." It was all she could think of at the moment. The air was pressing in on her. It was as if the whole world had suddenly tilted. She had to get out. She had to read this paper.

"I'll deal," Farley said. "Just tell Samuel Wallace his fancy gambling woman can't handle it anymore."

"S'right," Sneaky Pete seconded, "always knew it wasn't no job a chippy could handle."

"I'll tell Samuel that you are dealing," Celia said, handing over the cards.

"Aw Red, now my luck's going to change," the soldier said. "Unless this is just my lucky night."

"I hope it is," Celia said. The hell with it, she thought. She asked the soldier, "Has Major Newcomb been around today? Or that other one, Fox?"

The soldier smiled, showing teeth scattered in his head between blackened stumps. "So far, it's been my lucky day," he told her. "Them two left from the fort about sundown ago and didn't show up here." He spat out the side of his mouth, "And if'n they do, I'll leave. The major and me have a little disagreement about the way I polish my boots."

"You know where they went?" Celia asked. Her voice quavered. What if the major went to kill Big Lil before Glidinghawk and Davis could get to her? And where was Fox? She'd feel a damned sight better when he brought her a pistol.

"Aw, the major said he was taking Fox out for some sabre practice, north of town. Haw—at night? There's some of us would rather desert than have sabre practice with the major." He spat again. "But that lieutenant, his nose is brown from sticking it up the major's bung hole—no offense, lady—so't be too much to hope he'd get his. . . ."

Celia's stomach felt like it had dropped off a cliff. She felt hollow inside. She could picture the fresh-faced Fox refusing to believe that his hero, the major, was a thoroughly dangerous man. She could picture him going to the major with what Glidinghawk had told him. She could see the major smiling that cruel, thin-lipped smile. . . .

"Red, you all right?" the soldier asked.

"No . . . yes. Do you have any idea where they are? It's awfully late. . . ."

The soldier pressed his lips together sullenly. "Heard the major and you got together last night, but I thought more of you, Red. Didn't think he was your type."

"Save the sermons, soldier. Have you any idea just where they are?"

Another enlisted man from the Sixth Cavalry volunteered, "There's an old homestead 'bout three miles up the trail, mostly blowed down. Talk is the major goes out there. You know where I mean, by the stand of trees don't rightly belong in these parts?"

Celia thought. She had a vague idea. Black Jack had mentioned that some fool had tried to start a ranch. It was not too far from where they had made their picnic.

She nodded, "I think I know. Thanks, soldier. And good luck."

She fled across the gambling hall, remembering she had promised to let Samuel know she was leaving. She wanted to run. She had to do something. Fox was in danger—if he wasn't already dead, his flesh sliced to ribbons.

Most of the whores looked away when Celia walked by. They could no longer afford to be friendly with her. Colored Susan nodded distantly, a gesture more like a plea for Celia to leave her alone.

Celia would get no help from any of them. They were owned by Madam Agnes, and somehow that meant the major also had a hold on them.

She crossed behind the bar to Samuel's office. She saw

202

him slumped at his desk in the counting room. Thank God. Slumped and inebriated. His glazed eyes tried to focus while spittle pooled on his mustache. "Celia?" he slurred.

If he couldn't sit up straight, Celia figured, he couldn't do her much harm. He was beyond knowing what was happening. This was her first bit of luck today. She leaned against the wall while Samuel leered at her drunkenly. She took the paper from her pocket.

Samuel mumbled something, tried to rise, and slumped back again.

Celia read quickly. The crumpled note was terse. It was written in Black Jack's scrawled hand. A message from the grave pointing the finger at his killers. Goosebumps raised on Celia's skin.

She scanned quickly. The few words burned a message into her brain as indelibly as a branding iron.

Landrum and the swamper, Texas Rangers or Federal Marshals? Celia???

So Black Jack had figured out that the three of them were here to clean up the Flats. Or two of them. The numerous question marks after her name meant he wasn't sure she was one of them.

The other words were also names. Names linked by marriage and blood. It was so simple. Everything fit. This was the jackpot.

Samuel Wallace and Agnes (Newcomb) Wallace, nominal owners of practically every plat—and whore-house—in the Flats. Major Bernard Newcomb, actual owner. Nellie (Vernon) Newcomb, his lawful wife."

"Wanna have some fun?" Samuel asked, trying to raise his head.

Celia looked at him coldly. She remembered all the

times she had endured his pawing and lecherous smiles. He was not the dangerous one, he was only a very weak man, a figurehead for the club and the property ownership. But he was detestable. And it would be nice to have him solidly out of commission.

"Sure, Sam," Celia said, striding to where he leaned, sideways, in his chair. "How about a kiss you'll remember for a long, long time?"

The smile on his face was lopsided and wet with spittle. He raised his head. Celia braced herself, drew back her fist, and planted a blow squarely on his chin. He slumped back in his chair, the smile still plastered across his sallow face.

Celia felt a rush of satisfaction, then remembered she still had a lot to do. She propped Wallace's body back up across the counting desk, rubbed her sore hands together briskly, and walked back into the club. Ten paces to her right, eyes straight ahead, and she was out the side door.

Celia heard voices behind her, but she ignored them. She had no great love for that little prig Fox, but if there was a chance he was still alive, she knew she had to try to reach him.

The night was heavy with storms that had not yet broken. Revelers wandered the streets looking for excitement. Celia thought of the murders, the disease, the robberies and beatings. They would find excitement all right. She slipped by them like a wraith.

The livery was five blocks down from the Bee Hive, on the side of the rutted street opposite the Brazos Club. She needed a good, swift horse. She felt in her handbag. The knife was still there. She tested the razor-sharp blade with her finger. It was all she had.

She knew the night guard at the livery. Ambrose was a

skinny man with a harelip who was the butt of town jokes. Because he talked funny, people said he was slow, but good with horses.

Once, some rowdy hardcases had dragged him into the club and gotten the best of him in a chug-a-lug contest. Ambrose had gotten sick. Celia had loaned him her handkerchief, helped clean him up, and told him to go home. She hoped she would not have to hurt him tonight.

The wide, barnlike doors abutting the street were shut tightly. Inside, Celia knew, Ambrose used one of the stalls for a bed. She walked cautiously around the back, looking for another entrance. Every step she took sounded loudly in her ears.

Horses neighed and whinnied.

There had to be a back entrance. It was dark. She felt her way along the rough planks. The ripe smell of horse manure assailed her nostrils.

"'Ode it wight d'ere."

A rifle dug into Celia's ribs. She stopped, stock still, afraid to make a move. "Ambrose. It's me, Celia. Red. Don't shoot."

"What 'ou 'ant, Miss Wed?" he asked her. She felt the barrel of the rifle waver.

"Listen, Ambrose, please. I need a horse quickly—a fast horse with good night vision. I don't have time to explain now, but you have to help me."

Ambrose lowered his rifle and scratched his head. He was afraid this was a joke, and one that would get him in trouble. He liked Celia, but maybe she was just like the others, always making fun of him because he couldn't talk right.

She sensed his fears. She reached forward and touched him lightly on the arm. "You can trust me," she whispered. "I'll leave you all the money I have, twenty dollars at least. I don't want to get you in trouble, but this is a matter of life and death. You must help."

Celia knew that women had never been kind to this man. She knew that his disfigured face and nasal speech made him a laughingstock. She made a split-second decision.

Ambrose was not stupid. If she let him know a little, if she appealed to his sense of manhood, maybe she would not have to use the knife—not that she expected to do much good with it, up against his rifle.

"I know who the killer of the Flats is, and he is about to strike again. You can be a hero. Get me a horse and loan me your rifle. And don't tell anyone."

"Aw, I'd 'ike to. . . ."

"Right now!" Celia said. "Or it will be too late, and it will be your fault."

He stood silently, still considering. Celia was impatient. She could almost see the thoughts tumbling around in his head. She was about to go for her knife when he said, "Aw 'ight."

Ten minutes later she was saddled up on a big sorrel, heading out of town. She carried Ambrose's rifle. It was an old, rusty single-action Spencer, but better than nothing.

There had been one bad moment, when Celia demanded Ambrose's britches, but by then Celia was holding his rifle on him. She hoped she could make it up to him. Ambrose was left in his underwear.

She walked the horse, alert for any untoward movements, fearing a volley of shots at any moment. She reassured herself that the major was not around, but that still left Madam Agnes and Nellie unaccounted for, and who knows who else might be an enemy? Celia was spooked.

From a distance, in the dark, she looked like a man. But even a man riding out this time of night was mighty suspicious.

Spurring the sorrel as she got further away from the livery and the fancy saloons, Celia galloped down the alley leading out of town.

The pigpens were in full swing, their interiors lit by lantern light. Down by Arlene's, she heard the crack of pistols and the screech of panicked women.

A blazing flame licked up to the sky. Celia wheeled her horse to a halt and watched as the flame danced higher, shooting sparks that fell on the adjoining shanties and caught.

The night sky began to glow.

Half-clad men and women swarmed into the alley like ants, shouting and running. Celia looked for Davis or Glidinghawk or Big Lil, but she could not distinguish any individual faces in the melee.

There was nothing she could do there.

But there might be something she could do if she caught up with Fox and Newcomb. She headed the sorrel due north and started to ride as if the devil himself were after her.

In fact, Celia thought wildly as the first forks of lightning split the sky wide open, she was riding out to meet the devil himself—alone and poorly armed. And she might already be too late.

CHAPTER TWENTY-ONE

The horse faltered once and slid into a mudhole. Celia held her seat and prayed. The horse whinnied, righted himself, and recovered. They moved on.

The abandoned ranch was not far now. The old Mueller place, Celia remembered, is what people called it. They laughed when they talked about it, that bitter dry laugh they used for people who could not survive their dreams. The Muellers had been gone five years or more.

The shell of the house remained. Celia saw it when the sky lit up with lightning. She was terrified of the lightning, but it also lit her way. Without it, she wouldn't make it.

Celia strained against the wind. She squinted, hair whipping her face. A blue-white shock of total illumination, then pitch black, except for a glow from what was left of the house. The sky rumbled. Someone was there.

Half of the house was rubble, windows blown out, walls tumbled. A twister had done that, folks said. It had not been rebuilt.

Gnarled trunks and branches from the stand of trees the soldier had mentioned groaned in the wind. They stood like skeletons to the left of the battered structure.

Celia dismounted. She led the horse the last hundred yards toward the trees and hoped the major was not staring out into the night. The electric flashes were coming closer together, flickering like a giant lantern.

After tying the horse, Celia crouched down and crept along toward the ruins, dragging the Spencer with her. The gun was loaded. She had extra shells with her. She had the knife. Both weapons seemed very frail and powerless.

Celia thought she heard the beat of horses' hooves in the distance, but she couldn't be sure. A fork of light sizzled. Thunder exploded in her ears.

She eased her way over the rubble. The old window was there, in the part of the house that had withstood other storms. She flattened herself against the wall and stood beside it.

Her ears rang. The wind got louder. Dead branches crackled to earth. From inside the fallen house came the dim glow of a lantern and a man's angry voice: the major.

There was another voice—higher, lighter. A woman's voice. Laughter. Insane laughter. Nellie? And the other voice . . . hoarse, pleading?

Celia hoped the voice belonged to Fox. At the very least, that would mean he was still alive. She edged closer. She could not hear what they were saying against the rising fury of the storm. Another inch. She pressed her spine into the wall. She angled her head. She looked inside.

Terror froze her to the spot.

Fox was lashed to a chair between Nellie and Major Newcomb. The major was in a trance, smiling. His lips made a thin, cruel line that cut across his enraptured face. A sabre glinted in his hand.

Nellie pirouetted in front of Fox. Her hands were on the lieutenant's uniform, running over the gaping wound that marred the clean cut of Fox's uniform. She held them up to Newcomb. Her fingers dripped with blood.

Beads of sweat popped out on Fox's forehead. His hands and legs were bound. The slicing wound had missed his lungs and heart, cutting a furrow along his right side, below the breastbone. He was fully conscious.

Celia realized with horror that they did not want to kill him quickly. They were playing with him the way a cat plays with a mouse. There was more laughter. The major's deep chuckle curdled Celia's blood.

Newcomb dug the gleaming point of the sabre into Fox's jacket, slicing through it with the sharp, deadly sword. The major twisted the sabre and sliced downward. His movements were swift and precise. The sturdy uniform fabric ribboned to Fox's waist. The bared flesh underneath was only nicked.

Nellie clapped her hands together and laughed louder.

Fox blanched and his head rolled back in animal terror.

Celia had seen enough. She readied the Spencer. Major Newcomb and Nellie were transfixed by Fox's tortured body. They did not see her. She eased herself up and poked the rifle barrel through the open window, lining Newcomb in the sights. Nellie's gaze was attracted by the dull gleam of metal. She screamed.

Newcomb dodged to the right as Celia pulled the trigger. The recoil knocked her backwards. She tripped over a dislodged brick. The bullet missed its mark. The blast echoed loudly. Nellie shrieked.

Celia tried to get her feet. One ankle gave way under

211

her. She reached for a fresh cartridge. Her fingers trembled. The rusty rifle needed oil. She could not work the lever. Suddenly arms grabbed her from behind. The rifle was torn from her grasp and flew through the air. Newcomb's weight pinned her to the ground.

Celia clawed at his face. She bit and kicked. But he was too strong. He dragged her along the ground, fighting to keep from being blown away. He hit her on the side of the head and swore.

They made the shelter of the standing northeast walls. Debris whirled around them. Fox's chair had toppled and, limbs bound, he clawed his way toward the corner. Nellie aimed a kick at his groin. A gust of wind stopped her leg in midair, bending it like a pretzel.

Newcomb reached for his sabre. Celia slithered from his grasp. He lashed out, but she sank to the ground. She pushed Fox to the wall, which wavered as if it were made of paper. Part of the roof collapsed on the spot where he had just been.

Nellie's constant shrieks were soon lost in the shrieking of a tornado. Celia could not see where Nellie went. Newcomb did not try to save her. He huddled beside the wall, clutching his sabre; Fox lay by his feet.

A shingle traveling at incredible speed rammed into Celia's shoulder. It stunned her. Fox sobbed. The chair that imprisoned him threatened to catapult skyward, carrying him along with it.

Celia crashed into him and fumbled for the restraining ropes. Her clumsy fingers tugged at the strong hemp. She remembered the knife that she had strapped to her left leg. It seemed to take forever to reach it.

Newcomb was watching her. He made no move, just

watched with a strange, exultant look in his eyes. His lips drew away from his teeth. They were bared in a grin like nothing Celia had ever seen before.

Finally, knife in hand, she slashed at Fox's ropes. Every movement took great effort. The hemp was thick and resilient. Fox's arms were twisted behind his back. At last, the final threads of rope gave. His hands were free. She knelt over him and went for the rope securing his ankles. She stabbed him once, but the rope gave.

Fox shrugged himself free of the chair, which was still tipped on its side. It skittered away from him, levitated, and crashed into a pile of rubble.

Weakened by his ordeal, Fox dragged his wounded body along the ground, reaching out with stiff hands. Major Newcomb calmly stood up to his full height above Fox as the wind suddenly abated.

Newcomb's eyes were transfixed, looking down on Fox and Celia, but beyond them. He raised his sabre up high, ceremoniously, with military precision.

Terror had rooted Fox to the ground. Newcomb's powerful arms lifted and held in midair. One sweep downward, and he would decapitate Fox. Another plunge, and Celia's prone body would be forever pinned to the earth.

The major had them in his power, gripped by a lust more powerful than sex.

Newcomb made only one mistake.

In an effort to hold on to his intense passion, to prolong his final ecstasy, he held his weapon poised and deadly above them. He waited for them to slaver and beg. He waited a second too long.

A shot slammed through his brain. The look on his face

was terrifying in its exultation. A round hole the size of a twenty-dollar gold piece exploded above his gleaming eyes.

He staggered backward, sabre still raised, and fell. The lethal blade clattered out of his death grip, piercing Fox's buttocks before coming to rest beside Celia. She stared at it for a long time before comprehending.

Fox passed out.

Landrum Davis came half crouching, half running toward them. Glidinghawk was beside him. Davis rolled Fox over gently, probing for critical wounds.

It was minutes before Celia could say anything. Oddly, she found herself sobbing into Glidinghawk's arms. Then she sobbed into Davis' arms. Finally, she sobbed and laughed.

"Fox?" she asked, when her emotions had spent. "Is he all right?"

"He's alive, if that's what you mean," Landrum said. "He'll have trouble sitting down for a while, but I can't think of anyone who deserves it more. Damned nuisance. Almost got us all killed."

Glidinghawk added, "I talked to him this afternoon. Told him about everything we suspected. All I can figure is he brought it to the major. . . ."

"Everything?" Celia asked quietly.

"The whole kit and kaboodle," Davis said. "Or enough to get your friend Annie killed. Glidinghawk found her, hacked up like Black Jack."

Fox stirred. He looked at Celia, then Davis, then Glidinghawk. Celia had tears in her eyes. The men looked cold as a Kansas winter.

"I didn't tell Newcomb everything," Fox said. "I only

told him enough to give him a chance to explain about his sister Agnes and the pigpens. He brought me out here. Nellie was waiting. She helped him. They . . . they enjoyed it. The more they hurt me, the more they liked it. But I wouldn't tell him about any of you, or who we were working for. . . ."

"It doesn't amount to a hill of beans now anyway," Davis said grimly. "They're both dead, and this is a helluva mess."

Fox sat up. His wounds were not bleeding heavily. "It makes a difference to me," he said. "I made a serious error in judgment. I am grateful to you for saving my life. But I would have gone to my grave without breaking your cover. I followed my orders."

Glidinghawk turned his back and spat.

Celia said, "I believe you, Fox. I saw some of it."

"I don't know if I can repay you," Fox said.

"I doubt it," Landrum said laconically.

"But I have some ideas," Fox continued. "Let me take Newcomb's body into town. That way it will not incriminate any of you. I can make it look like another of the Flats' murders. . . ."

Davis nodded, but appeared unconvinced. "That makes sense, but how are you going to get him back there without help? And there's Nellie's body, too. We tripped over it on the way in. Only good thing is half the town is burned down and things are about as confused as a herd of bulls let loose with one cow."

"The pigpens," Celia recalled aloud.

"You burned the pigpens?" Fox asked, his voice rising to a squeal. "And how do I log that in my report? Burned property? Our orders said to clean up the

215

pigpens, but. . . ."

"Didn't plan it like it happened, but we had a little trouble getting Big Lil out of that whorehouse down there."

Celia had been afraid to ask, after hearing about Annie. Annie, who wanted nothing but to get along in life without no man and without no trouble. "Is Lil all right?"

"She is now," Glidinghawk said, "but I'm not sure about my mustang. Big Lil has a little more heft than he's used to. We left her in camp."

"The tornado," Celia wailed.

"We almost couldn't get to you. We had to wait it out when it hit here. It started to the north and veered off east. Big Lil might be wet and miserable, but she should be all right," Landrum reported.

"What do we do now?" Celia asked. She wished she could sink into a soft bed. She wished she never had to see the Flats again.

Landrum stood by her and patted her on the shoulder. "Just a few more hours and we can all get out of here. The three of us deserve a cushy assignment after this, eh, Fox?"

Fox was about to say something, but he changed his mind. They rehearsed their roles. Fox could walk, though not comfortably. He and Glidinghawk would cart the corpses to town. They would be dumped in an alley. Fox would find them.

Davis would head back to camp to take care of Big Lil, since she had important evidence on Agnes and Newcomb. He seemed to be looking forward to it.

Fox would have to lie for all of them.

The lieutenant listened and nodded. He agreed to

216

everything. He would tell people that Nellie was a killer, working with Samuel Wallace. Fox would say that Nellie and the major got in an argument and ended up killing each other.

Then Fox would contact the Texas Rangers and the Adjutant General's office. Agnes Newcomb Wallace and her husband Samuel would be charged as accessories in the murders at the Flats. Agnes would be charged with the murder of Annie Downey. The charges, and the fact that most of their property burned up, would put them out of business.

Celia's part in the charade was over. She was to go back to her hotel, gather her belongings and take Ben Ficklin's Mail and Stage Line out of town the following day. Davis and Glidinghawk would meet up with her later. She did not have to go back to the Brazos Club.

For her, it was over. Almost.

"What are you going to do with Black Jack's money?" Fox asked.

"What money?" Celia asked. She had figured it had long since disappeared.

Fox got that priggish look on his face. "The money on Newcomb. He's carrying what's left of what he took from Black Jack. Isn't that what you really came after?"

Glidinghawk whirled Fox around so hard that the lieutenant's wounds reopened. The Indian stared down at the man who had almost gotten Celia killed. Fox dropped his eyes and looked at the ground. He didn't have to be told.

"I did not mean it that way, Celia. You are a very brave woman and I'm proud to be on your team." He almost choked on his words, but he said them.

Celia nodded absently, thinking of what the pot had

really bought Black Jack. She remembered his plans to own a fancy place in the Flats.

"Give it to Big Lil," she said decisively. "Tell her to open up the fanciest, straightest whorehouse in town."

Fox's eyes bugged out and his face turned red, but he had the good sense to keep his mouth shut. There was nothing more to be said.

CHAPTER TWENTY-TWO

Amos Powell sat behind his wide oak desk. He was tense. The report from 2nd Lt. Fox had just arrived by special messenger. It was marked CONFIDENTIAL and sealed with red wax. Knowing that this was either the end—or a new beginning—for Powell's Army, Amos' fingers trembled slightly as he broke the seal, extracted the pages, and proceeded to read:

To: Lt. Col. Amos Powell
Adjutant General
US Army Territorial Command
Fort Leavenworth, Kansas

From: 2nd Lt. Preston Kirkwood Fox
Fort Griffin, Texas

The case at Fort Griffin can be officially closed. In cooperation with Operatives *A*, *B*, and *C*, I have ascertained that the man behind the murders at Fort Griffin was one Major Bernard Newcomb, Commander, US Army Post, Fort Griffin. Major Newcomb, in conspiracy with his sister Madam

Agnes Newcomb and brother-in-law Samuel Wallace, nominal owners and operators of The Brazos Club, was the real owner of the most despicable pigpens in the Flats. Aided by his wife Nellie Vernon, a woman of the lowest sort, Major Newcomb murdered his striker Seth Downey, who had discovered the truth about him, as well as numerous enlisted men and the civilian gambler known as Black Jack, to whom I referred in previous communiques.

In view of the sensitive nature of this revelation, it is scarcely regrettable that while I was confronting the Major with these truths, aided by Operatives *A*, *B*, and *C*, the natural disaster of a tornado intervened, killing Nellie Vernon. The Major, alas, was killed in the fracas that ensued, after threatening bodily harm to us all. Because the bodies were removed to the Flats, and there discovered in a manner suggesting a lover's quarrel, the good name of the US Army can be fully protected and I am recommending no posthumous court-martial.

As Samuel Wallace and Madam Agnes Wallace, whom I have reported to both the federal sheriff and the Texas Rangers, are civilians, the official blame for the corruption of the pigpens as well as the murders that took place there rests squarely with them, a situation I trust you will find amenable. Both despicable creatures have fled, but Texas officials are in hot pursuit.

In closing, I should add that Operatives *A*, *B*, and *C* worked in a highly professional, if unorthodox, manner in this delicate matter. Although it is impossible to officially recognize and commend them, they have earned my personal commendation.

June 15, 1874   FOX

Poppycock, Amos thought. There was no doubt in Amos' mind that Fox owed his life to the others. Amos Powell looked forward to hearing Landrum's version of the case, or Glidinghawk's, or Celia's.

Still, it was too fine a day to waste carping. The main thing was that Powell's Army had won—and just in time to upset Pee Wee Hurst's applecart.

It was hard to argue against success. The proposed army budget cuts would not affect Amos' team of undercover operatives. He might even put in for a raise for them—that ought to raise a few eyebrows.

Amos placed the latest communication in the Powell's Army folder and closed it with a smile of satisfaction. He knew it was a job well done.

THE UNTAMED WEST
brought to you by Zebra Books

THE LAST MOUNTAIN MAN   (1480, $2.25)
by William W. Johnstone

He rode out West looking for the men who murdered his father
and brother. When an old mountain man taught him how to kill a
man a hundred different ways from Sunday, he knew he'd make
sure they all remembered . . . THE LAST MOUNTAIN MAN.

SAN LOMAH SHOOTOUT   (1853, $2.50)
by Doyle Trent

Jim Kinslow didn't even own a gun, but a group of hardcases
tried to turn him into buzzard meat. There was only one way to
find out why anybody would want to stretch his hide out to dry,
and that was to strap on a borrowed six-gun and ride to death or
glory.

TOMBSTONE LODE   (1915, $2.95)
by Doyle Trent

When the Josey mine caved in on Buckshot Dobbs, he left behind
a rich vein of Colorado gold — but no will. James Alexander,
hired to investigate Buckshot's self-proclaimed blood relations
learns too soon that he has one more chance to solve the mystery
and save his skin or become another victim of TOMBSTONE
LODE.

GALLOWS RIDERS   (1934, $2.50)
by Mark K. Roberts

When Stark and his killer-dogs reached Colby, all it took was a
little muscle and some well-placed slugs to run roughshod over
the small town — until the avenging stranger stepped out of the
shadows for one last bloody showdown.

DEVIL WIRE   (1937, $2.50)
by Cameron Judd

They came by night, striking terror into the hearts of the settlers.
The message was clear: Get rid of the devil wire or the land would
turn red with fencestringer blood. It was the beginning of a brutal
range war.

SPINE TINGLING HORROR
from Zebra Books

CHILD'S PLAY   (1719, $3.50)
by Andrew Neiderman
From the day the foster children arrived, they looked up to Alex. But soon they began to act like him—right down to the icy sarcasm, terrifying smiles and evil gleams in their eyes. Oh yes, they'd do anything to please Alex.

THE DOLL   (1788, $3.50)
by Josh Webster
When Gretchen cradled the doll in her arms, it told her things—secret, evil things that her sister Mary could never know about. For it hated Mary just as she did. And it knew how to get back at Mary . . . forever.

DEW CLAWS   (1808, $3.50)
by Stephen Gresham
The memories Jonathan had of his Uncle and three brothers being sucked into the fetid mud of the Night Horse Swamp were starting to fade . . . only to return again. It had taken everything he loved. And now it had come back—for him.

TOYS IN THE ATTIC   (1862, $3.95)
by Daniel Ransom
Brian's best friend Davey had disappeared and already his clothes and comic books had vanished—as if Davey never existed. Somebody was playing a deadly game—and now it was Brian's turn . . .

THE ALCHEMIST   (1865, $3.95)
by Les Whitten
Of course, it was only a hobby. No harm in that. The small alchemical furnace in the basement could hardly invite suspicion. After all, Martin was a quiet, government worker with a dead-end desk job. . . . Or was he?

SAIGON COMMANDOS
by Jonathan Cain

It is Vietnam as we've never seen it before, revealed with bitter reality and love — of a people and a place.

SAIGON COMMANDOS	(1283, $3.25)
#2: CODE ZERO: SHOTS FIRED!	(1329, $2.50)
#4: CHERRY-BOY BODY BAG	(1407, $2.50)
#5: BOONIE-RAT BODY BURNING	(1441, $2.50)
#6: DI DI MAU OR DIE	(1493, $2.50)
#7: SAC MAU, VICTOR CHARLIE	(1574, $2.50)
#8: YOU DIE, DU MA!	(1629, $2.50)
#9: MAD MINUTE	(1698, $2.50)
#10: TORTURERS OF TET	(1772, $2.50)
#11: HOLLOWPOINT HELL	(1848, $2.50)
#12: SUICIDE SQUAD	(1897, $2.50)